Praise for
No Way Never Sisters

"Funny and relatable . . . Acevedo and Sylvester will have you rooting for this family from day one, even as Meli and Roxy get more and more creative with their hijinks."
—Andrea Beatriz Arango, Newbery Honor Award–winning author of *Iveliz Explains It All*

"Weaving tried-and-true tropes with fresh scenarios and characterization, Acevedo and Sylvester deftly navigate the complicated aspects of family, chronic illness (Meli has scoliosis), changing relationships, and growing up, handling it all with heart and humor."
—*Kirkus Reviews*

"Effervescent . . . Throughout Meli and Roxy's distinct alternating perspectives, the authors sprinkle affecting moments of burgeoning sisterhood into comedic mishaps, imparting raw emotional resonance into the frothy anti-rom-com."
—*Publishers Weekly*

No Way Never Sisters

CHANTEL ACEVEDO & NATALIA SYLVESTER

ALADDIN
New York   Amsterdam/Antwerp   London
Toronto   Sydney/Melbourne   New Delhi

This book is a work of fiction. Any references to historical events, real people, or real places are used fictitiously. Other names, characters, places, and events are products of the author's imagination, and any resemblance to actual events or places or persons, living or dead, is entirely coincidental.

ALADDIN
An imprint of Simon & Schuster Children's Publishing Division
1230 Avenue of the Americas, New York, New York 10020
For more than 100 years, Simon & Schuster has championed authors and the stories they create. By respecting the copyright of an author's intellectual property, you enable Simon & Schuster and the author to continue publishing exceptional books for years to come. We thank you for supporting the author's copyright by purchasing an authorized edition of this book. No amount of this book may be reproduced or stored in any format, nor may it be uploaded to any website, database, language-learning model, or other repository, retrieval, or artificial intelligence system without express permission. All rights reserved. Inquiries may be directed to Simon & Schuster, 1230 Avenue of the Americas, New York, NY 10020
or permissions@simonandschuster.com.
First Aladdin hardcover edition March 2026
Text © 2026 by Chantel Acevedo and Natalia Sylvester
Illustrations © 2026 by Solène Debiès
Also available in an Aladdin paperback edition.
All rights reserved, including the right of reproduction in whole or in part in any form.
ALADDIN and related logo are registered trademarks of Simon & Schuster, LLC.
For information about special discounts for bulk purchases, please contact Simon & Schuster Special Sales at 1-866-506-1949 or business@simonandschuster.com.
Simon & Schuster strongly believes in freedom of expression and stands against censorship in all its forms. For more information, visit BooksBelong.com.
The Simon & Schuster Speakers Bureau can bring authors to your live event.
For more information or to book an event, contact the Simon & Schuster Speakers Bureau at 1-866-248-3049 or visit our website at www.simonspeakers.com.
Book design by Laura Lyn DiSiena and Ginny Chu
The text of this book was set in Perpetua.
Manufactured in the United States of America 0126 BVG
2 4 6 8 10 9 7 5 3 1
Library of Congress Cataloging-in-Publication Data
Names: Acevedo, Chantel author | Sylvester, Natalia author
Title: No way never sisters / by Chantel Acevedo and Natalia Sylvester.
Description: First Aladdin hardcover edition. | New York : Aladdin, 2026. | Audience: Ages 8 to 12 | Summary: "Two girls refuse to be related and try and keep their parents apart, only to find acceptance in the end"—Provided by publisher.
Identifiers: LCCN 2024061229 (print) | LCCN 2024061230 (ebook) |
ISBN 9781665974127 hardcover | ISBN 9781665974141 ebook
Subjects: CYAC: Stepfamilies—Fiction | Friendship—Fiction | LCGFT: Novels
Classification: LCC PZ7.1.A2148 No 2026 (print) | LCC PZ7.1.A2148 (ebook)
LC record available at https://lccn.loc.gov/2024061229
LC ebook record available at https://lccn.loc.gov/2024061230
ISBN 9781665974134 (pbk)

For my sister, Andrea,
with love always
—C. A.

To my big sister, Ushu
—N. S.

Part One:
Mi Casa NO Es Tu Casa

CHAPTER 1
MELI

Until several months ago, I could've counted on one hand the things I knew about Roxy Romero.

One: She was captain of the flag football team.

Two: She always got her way, like when she became our sixth-grade class president by a landslide, same as in fifth grade, and fourth.

Three: Our little brothers have the same name. Hers goes by Ben, mine goes by Benji, but everyone in third grade called them the Bens.

Four: Last year, Roxy stole my favorite purple pen. She "borrowed" it to sign everyone's yearbook, misspelled my name with two *S*'s, then never gave it back.

And five? I used to not have any other fun facts about Roxy Romero until one day, I learned a big one.

Five: Roxy's dad and my mom were dating.

So not fun. *So*, unfortunately, fact.

"Reservation under Carlos Romero, please. Party of six."

It was the last week of school and our parents had taken us to Bacio del Capo (*chef's kiss* in Italian), a fancy but casual restaurant where people ate like they were at home sharing the same main dish. That's what the website said, anyway. I'd read up on it on the way over because I wanted to know what to expect.

"Something's weird about this place," Roxy said as we followed the hostess to a large, round table in the corner of the room.

"They call it *family style*," I whispered. "It means we get our own dishes, silverware, and condiments from over there." I pointed to a counter with stacks of freshly washed plates against the wall. "And we 'make ourselves at home.'" I made air quotes with my fingers because those were the website's words, not mine.

"Oh. That's pretty cool, actually!"

This was easy for Roxy to say, since she actually had a home. Mine was all packed up in boxes. After my parents split last year, Mami decided we should sell the house. Papi had moved out long before the divorce was official, and he was always in another country, shooting travel documentaries for work. I'd known since I was little that my parents were happier people apart than as a couple, but still, sometimes my mind liked to play pretend. I'd imagine being part of a whole family again. In *our* house.

Roxy and her dad and Ben? They weren't exactly part of the fantasy.

I sighed. It's not like I hated Roxy. I just wasn't her number one fan like everyone else in our school. Even before our parents started dating, she and I didn't mix. Once, at Field Day, we got paired for the three-legged race, and we couldn't get in step to save our lives. I was yelling "Wait up!" and she was yelling "You got this!" when we tripped over each other into a big old pile of mud. Our parents came rushing to help, and that's how they met—their origin story was our literal downfall. Mami went all heart-eyes for Carlos after he helped me wobble off the field, and now they were constantly making us hang out. There was that time they signed us up for a volleyball tournament, but I got a random nosebleed before my feet even touched sand. Then they tried to make us bond over a pottery-making class, but Roxy's lump of clay catapulted off the wheel and landed right on top of the flower-shaped mug I was making for Mami.

We didn't even have each other's phone numbers because Roxy had never bothered asking me. We were polar opposites with nothing in common, but our parents wanted us to become BFFs. I already had those. James, Janette, and I had our own group chat because we'd been best friends *and* neighbors ever since we were in kindergarten.

Now that our house had finally sold, all that was about to change.

"There's always room for more friends," Mami loved to say. But I didn't want new friends, or a new house, or a replacement for Papi. I just wanted my old life back.

"You okay, Meli? You were so quiet on the way over," Mami said. "I thought you'd be excited to celebrate the new house."

That was Mami's favorite word lately: *excited*. She was all about looking on the bright side of things, acting like the big changes in our lives were happy ones. I knew she was just trying to keep me and Benji from being sad about missing Papi, so I tried to play along and not be a party pooper. Besides, real artists used art to express their complicated emotions. And I had a lot of those.

"I am excited. I was just . . . brainstorming ideas for my presentation. You know how distracted I get when inspiration strikes." The Summer Kickoff Talent Show was the biggest event of the school year, and I'd been working on my sculpture for months. This week I'd finally share it with everyone.

We took a seat. Mami sat annoyingly close to Carlos, Roxy and I sat next to each of our parents, and the Bens closed our circle by sitting side by side. Right away they opened the crayon boxes on the table and started playing tic-tac-toe on the paper place mats.

"The talent show? Trust me, don't stress it," Roxy said. "It's the last thing people will care about on the last day of school."

"*I* care about it. And who said anything about being stressed?" I'd been feeling pretty good about it, actually, until Roxy decided to diss it.

Roxy's jaw dropped, and she took in a quick breath. "Oh. I didn't mean it like that."

"Then how did you mean it?"

"Just that you'll be . . . never mind."

That was one of the new facts I'd learned about Roxy since our parents started dating.

Six: She didn't really think before she spoke.

"Okay then!" Roxy's dad clapped his hands together and set a giant iPad on the table. "Who wants to see pictures of the new house?"

Mami placed her hand over his. "Shouldn't we wait until after we eat? We never have screens during dinner."

It was true. Mami's rules were ironclad. For once, I was glad, because I'd seen the new house on Mami's phone and it was really old. And ugly. But Mami also had a rule about not being rude and always being nice if you can help it. So I'd flipped through the pictures and said the house looked vintage.

Carlos grinned, not even a little bit discouraged. "But Evy, I think the kids will be excited to see the surprise on the last slide."

Roxy leaned forward while I tried not to roll my eyes. It was probably something cheesy like a confetti meme or a video of Carlos moonwalking across our new kitchen. Roxy's dad had a way of treating any piece of good news like an excuse for a touchdown dance.

"Bueno, just this once," Mami said. I stiffened. Mami never made exceptions: not for me, or Benji, or my dad. Never, ever. What made Roxy's dad so special?

"Excellent," Carlos said, and pressed play. A slideshow with a cheery piano tune blasted from the speaker as image after image popped up. The house was boxy, with blue and white awnings and windows made of glass blocks that looked like ice cubes. It had orange ceramic roof tiles that were green from mold, and the backyard was full of overgrown banana trees. Who needed that much fruit?

"It's awesome," Ben said in a low, awestruck voice. "Like a wild jungle out of a story."

"Well, yes, the landscape is a little . . . overgrown," Mami said, just as the pictures switched to the inside, which wasn't in much better shape. "It's a fixer-upper, but it has good bones."

"Like a dinosaur!" Benji practically roared.

"Yes, hijito, like a dinosaur," Mami said.

"Except you can actually bring this one back to life," Roxy added.

Everyone laughed except for me. All I could think about was my old room. Two years ago, for my tenth birthday, Papi had taken me to the home improvement store and told me I could redecorate however I wanted. He filmed the before and after on his phone and made a mini documentary, our very own home makeover show. But now he was halfway across the world in Spain, shooting a documentary about history. My bedroom would soon be a memory I couldn't go back to.

"It's a cute house," Roxy said. "It has loads of potential."

"You sound like your dad," I said.

"Is that a bad thing?"

Maybe it was. This was Carlos's fault, after all. The *Miami Weekly* had voted him "Everyone's favorite family real estate agent," according to the ads I'd seen on bus benches. He's the one who helped my mom sell our old house and buy this new one.

"I just think it's easy to sell someone on a new house if you're not the one that has to live in it," I finally blurted.

"Meli! That's not nice," Mami said.

"Are you calling my dad a sellout?" Roxy scoffed.

Mami and Carlos looked so hurt that I felt like the world's biggest meanie. I tried to backtrack. "What?

No! What I meant was, Carlos is really good at what he does. He makes every house look amazing."

"Wow. That's so kind of you, Meli, thank you," Carlos said.

Way to overcorrect, Melisa. Carlos was a nice-enough guy, but what did I know about his job performance? I guess I'd just felt bad about being rude.

Mami glowed, grinning ear to ear. For months now, she'd been asking me question after question about Carlos: How do you like him? Isn't he great? How are you and Roxy getting along?

My answers were always more or less the same: *He seems cool. He's really something. Fine, same as always.*

Technically all of those things were true. Even though they weren't the rave reviews Mami clearly hoped for, they seemed to make her happy. After she and Papi divorced, Mami became so quiet and sad that I got into the habit of trying to cheer her up. Now Carlos was always the one doing that. And tonight, Mami was bubbly with joy.

"You're right, Meli. Carlos always outdoes himself. In fact, kids, something really special happened this afternoon. When we finally got the keys to the house . . ."

"We made things official!" Carlos swiped the screen to the next slide. It was a picture of keys in a jewelry box, right next to . . . a diamond ring?!

"No way. You're getting married?" Roxy nearly jumped out of her chair, and the boys started cheering.

My throat went dry. My mind became an echo chamber of *no, no, no, no, no!* All I managed to say was, "Wait, does this mean the new house—"

"Is going to be our new home! For all of us!" Mami said.

"And we're going to fix it up just in time for the wedding at the end of the summer!" Carlos added.

"Yesssss!" Benji said. "This is the best day ever." He jumped up and hugged my mom and then Carlos, and soon they were all having their own little lovefest. I wished I could slip below the table, never to be found again. Roxy slouched in her chair, looking like her flag football team had just lost zero to a hundred.

"¿Chicas?" Mami suddenly remembered we existed. "We thought you'd be happy."

Carlos offered his hand to Roxy. "You always said you wanted a sister."

We locked eyes and waited to see what the other would say.

"Buona sera, everyone!" A cheerful waitress with a name tag that said JULIA greeted us in exaggerated Italian. "What can I get you all to drink?"

"Um . . ." Roxy blinked like she'd just woken up from a nightmare. "I'd like a Sprite, please." I waited for Mami to interrupt. *Soda on a weeknight?* No way. But she was too busy taking her engagement ring out of her purse to notice.

"And for your sister?" Julia asked.

"We're not sisters," we both snapped.

"Jinx!" the Bens sang.

"Stop it!" we said in sync again. We gasped and turned to each other. "Now you're just—"

I stopped talking.

"—doing it on purpose," Roxy said.

"*Not* sisters. Got it. I'll be back with your drink orders!" Julia said. She was gone before I could ask for an apple juice.

"Well, this is off to an interesting start," Carlos said, raising his eyebrows at Mami.

"How could she confuse us for sisters? We look nothing alike," Roxy said.

It was true. Roxy had light brown wavy hair that stopped at her shoulders, while mine was straight, brownish black, and braided halfway down my back. She had a mist of freckles over her nose (Mami always said they were *so cute*), whereas all I had was a dimple on my left cheek. Everything about us was opposite: Roxy's features were sharp but mine were round; she was always dressed sporty but I liked more flowy, boho styles. Plus, I was at least three inches taller than her.

"Indeed. Chicas, why don't you go grab us some plates and silverware while we decide what we want to order for our first meal as a family?"

Roxy's chair screeched as she got up. "Can we get spaghetti and meatballs?"

"I'd like the lasagna, please," I said.

Mami put her hands in the air like it wasn't her decision. "It's all meat and red sauce and pasta, no matter how you slice it."

"This is bananas," Roxy said as we walked away. "They expect us all to live together when we can't even agree on dinner?"

I agreed but I didn't say so. The restaurant had gotten loud. There was a musician going table to table with an accordion, and a photographer taking group pictures of customers. Pots and pans clanged and steam hissed out of the kitchen. It made me feel trapped. I decided to focus on our task instead.

"Here. I'll get the big plates, you carry the salad plates," I said, handing her a small stack of six porcelain dishes before picking up the dinner plates.

"Why? We can each just use one plate." Roxy placed the smaller plates back on the counter. "Less mess."

"No, Mami always uses a separate plate for the salad."

"That's silly. Changing it up for once won't hurt her."

I piled the plates onto my stack this time. "Well, maybe my mom doesn't *want* any more big changes in her life."

Roxy started trying to take the small stack back. "Well, maybe she should try loosening up a little!"

I had a feeling we weren't talking about the plates anymore.

"Maybe no one ever asked for your opinion!" I said, snatching them out of her reach.

"Well mayb—"

Crashhhh.

All twelve dishes fell to the floor, their pieces shattering at our feet. The restaurant got super quiet, then erupted into applause and laughter. Roxy brought her hands to her forehead and started breathing real fast. I felt like my face was on fire, and my cheeks tingled like when you hold back a sneeze.

"Oh no. What did you do?" she said.

"*Me?* You're the one who dropped the plates because you weren't getting your way."

"My way? Ha! Moving in with you just because our parents got engaged is definitely not my way." Roxy's eyes formed tiny slits, sharp as a paper cut as she looked at me. Right then and there, I decided I'd learned two new things about her.

Seven: Roxy Romero was *not* my friend.

Eight: There was *no way* she was going to be my sister.

"Girls! Are you okay?" Carlos ran up behind us lightning fast.

"Ay, no," Mami said when she caught up to us. "Where's the manager? We're going to need you girls to apologize."

I could tell she was really upset, but then by some miracle the manager said no apology was necessary. He actually laughed and led us back to our table while the crew cleaned up. "In parts of Italy, breaking plates is a New Year's tradition. It represents getting rid of the old and making room for the new! You did us a favor six months ahead of time!"

"Is that so?" Mami said, pinching my chin.

I blinked away hot tears. This was exactly what

I was afraid of. It was bad enough that Mami had sold our house and I'd no longer live near my best friends, but now we'd have to fix up the new one, move in with the Romeros, and deal with the chaos of wedding planning, all in the summer before seventh grade. Why did everything have to break just for us to start over?

"Let's keep the celebration going!" Julia said as she brought everyone but me their drinks. She signaled for the photographer to come to our table and our parents squished us all together.

"Say *famiglia*!" the photographer said.

The boys' faces broke into cheesy grins. Roxy curled her lips without showing any teeth. My smile felt stiff and fake, like it'd been plastered onto my mouth.

The camera flashed once, then twice. "That's going straight into the family album!" Carlos said.

Us, a family? I didn't want to picture it. Not now, not ever.

CHAPTER 2
ROXY

Leave it to my cheesy dad and his uptight girlfriend, er, *fiancée*, to upend my whole life with only a week to go before school ended for the summer. Everyone knows the last week of school is the best week of school. Teachers either show movies in their classes or give us "free time." The nice ones bring cupcakes, and the mean ones are so eager to get away for the summer that they spend the whole week stripping bulletin boards, emptying file cabinets, and ignoring their students.

It should have been great, except I couldn't sleep all week thinking about Dad and Evy's plans. I tossed and turned every night, my brain churning with everything that could happen. Would Evy force me and Ben to follow all her rules? Would she make me and Meli wear matching outfits in family photos? Would Dad start to like Meli more than me?

The questions would pop up in my mind like that Whack-a-Mole game at the fair. Again and again they came, and it didn't matter how ridiculous I knew the questions were. My therapist, Dr. Nordan, calls these thoughts *ruminating*, but I call them my mental jump scares, and sometimes I can't make them stop.

Dr. Nordan tells me not to fight the questions. "Let them come, Roxy. Imagine they are little waves at the beach. Ride the waves. They'll calm on their own," she says.

But sometimes, no matter how much I try to relax, the waves just don't stop.

When Friday finally rolled around, I was starting to feel better. Friday was the last day of classes before summer, and the Summer Kickoff Talent Show was going to start right after the first bell of the day. More importantly, my birthday had arrived at last!

"Happy birthday!" Dad and Ben shouted as I came into the kitchen that morning. Dad held up a stack of chocolate chip pancakes and Ben handed me a homemade card with a drawing of me scoring a touchdown on the front and a big heart on the inside.

We all sat and ate our fill, washing everything down with chocolate milk, because it was my birthday and sugar was on the menu. "So, kiddo, are you ready for the talent show?"

"Mm-hmm," I said, my mouth full of pancake. I pointed at the bright red box in the corner. "I'm doing a one-girl skit about riding a roller coaster," I said after swallowing. I'd made the coaster out of a moving box I'd found in the garage. There were a bunch of them, empty and stacked in a corner by my bike. Dad said they were for our "Big Move."

Ben got up to examine my coaster. "It's great! I'll bet Meli's presentation is going to be awesome too," he said.

"Not cool, Ben," I muttered under my breath. I mean, why bring *her* up? He was probably right, though. Meli was a talented artist. Even her handwriting was beautiful. It didn't matter what her project looked like, though. Mine *meant* something. It wasn't just awesome looking (though it was) or neatly painted (because it wasn't).

Maybe Dad and I would be the only ones who understood the real meaning behind my skit, but that would be okay. The great thing about roller coasters is that they make my brain hush up for a while. At my first visit, Dr. Nordan explained that some people had quiet minds.

"You mean to tell me some people can just sit there . . . in silence?" I'd asked Dr. Nordan.

"Exactly. Some people's brains don't whir and buzz with nonstop questions, fears, and plans, Roxy," Dr. Nordan likes to remind me.

The buzzing grew worse after Mom left. She and Dad had broken up when I was five and Ben was two. Up until January, my brother and I would spend every other week at Mom's, then we'd go to Dad's house. Then Mom went to live with my abuelo in New Jersey for help with her depression. "Just for a little while," she'd promised. But it was nearly summer vacation and she was still there. I know that Abuelo is taking care of her, and that she's working hard to get better and come back home. But even so, it's scary to wonder whether my mom is okay or not. I can't help but think about it. And think about it. And think about it.

Dr. Nordan says that some worrying is normal, but that if *all* I do is worry, then I should try a different approach. She suggests I try to think of my worrisome thoughts as the part of my brain that tries *too hard* to be helpful. She says I should tell it, "Shh. Thank you, but I'm okay." It doesn't always work. Sometimes I imagine a little goblin in my head yelling at me. On busy days, when I'm distracted, the goblin sounds small and far away, and I hardly hear it. Other times, it's like she's shouting all her worries in my ear. That's what happened when Meli made us drop the plates at the restaurant. *Look what you did*, the goblin screeched. *Everyone will hate you now.*

As it turned out, my twelfth birthday was one bad-luck moment after another. It started when Dad got a flat tire on the way to school. He pulled the car over to the side of the road in front of a house with a row of palm trees that scratched the sky. It was hot already and I could feel my armpits getting sweaty.

"It'll be okay, kiddos," he said, rummaging in the trunk for the car jack, then immediately banging his head on the top of the trunk.

"That's reassuring," I muttered. Eventually, Evy came by to make sure we were okay after dropping off Meli and Benji at school.

"Feliz cumple, Roxy!" Evy said, giving me a tight hug. Then, I had to wait five long, excruciating minutes while the two of them stared all lovey-dovey into each other's eyes and spoke in whispers before Evy said: "Hop in, kids. I'll give you a ride to school."

"Finally," I groaned, low enough for nobody to hear me. Evy popped the trunk of her car, and we loaded my cardboard roller coaster inside.

"Qué lindo te quedó," Evy said, complimenting my project.

"Thanks."

"Meli made a very special art piece. You should

ask her to tell you about it. You know how shy she can be."

I didn't say anything. Was Meli shy? We'd known each other since kindergarten, but we were never in class together after that year, when they separated the gifted kids from the regular classes. She didn't seem shy, at least not when she was with her best friends, James and Janette. The three of them went everywhere together, ate lunch at their own table, had side by side lockers, and wore group Halloween costumes every year. They were Dorothy, the Scarecrow, and the Cowardly Lion last year. Guess which one Meli was?

Dorothy. The main character. Definitely not the shy type. But the cliquish type? Absolutely. In fact, one time I borrowed Meli's purple pen to sign her yearbook, and when I gave the book back to her, I accidentally forgot to return the pen. When I doubled back to hand it over, the three of them stared icicle missiles at me with their eyes. I panicked, left the room, and threw the pen into the closest garbage can.

Seriously. Shy, my butt.

The car ride was silent. Uncomfortably silent, in fact. Sometimes being quiet with other people is completely okay, like when you're watching TV, or when you're in class. And sometimes it's weird and awful. The goblin in my brain kept saying one thing over and over again—*Evy is thinking about you right now*.

This time, the goblin was right.

"Twelve today, right?" Evy said. She glanced at the rearview mirror to look at me.

"Yup."

"We'll have to celebrate, then!" Evy said, grinning at me in the mirror.

"Yeah, sure." I vowed to ask Dad if he'd take me to the movies. Just me and him and Ben. A Romeros-only night out, please and thank you.

"Here we are," Evy announced, pulling into my school's driveway. She scribbled a note about the flat tire on a piece of paper and gave it to me to take to the attendance office. "Your dad put me on your emergency contact card."

When had *that* happened? I imagined Evy taking me and Ben to the doctor for our checkups. Evy making our lunches. Evy, sitting there in her pajamas on Christmas morning. Meli would be there too.

Meli would be all over my future from now on.

Get it together, I told myself again. *One problem at a time.* That was another Dr. Nordan tip. "If thinking doesn't lead to a solution," she always says, "then it's just worrying. Take one problem at a time."

Evy would drop Ben off at his school next. I waved goodbye to him, retrieved my project from the trunk of Evy's car, and ran as fast as I could into the school. I struggled with my roller coaster through the halls, bumping the corners every so often, and stopped at my locker.

My jaw dropped.

Taped to my locker were twelve helium-filled balloons, one from each member of the flag football team. They'd drawn silly faces on the balloons and hung a sign above my locker that read:

HAPPY BIRTHDAY, QUARTERBACK!

Quarterback? I was going to be *quarterback* next year? Talk about a great birthday gift!

An idea popped into my mind. I grabbed the balloons. They would represent the other passengers. I could see it now—I'd be up on stage, sitting inside my cardboard vehicle, with twelve "friends" bobbing beside me. Loaded with the box and the balloons, I ran straight to the cafetorium.

"Slow down!" Mr. Padrón shouted at me as I zipped past him.

The talent show was already underway when I got there. Everyone turned to look at me as I wrestled the balloons and box through the cafetorium doors. Meli was on stage, presenting her art piece, which looked like a seashell tower that was almost as tall as her. Seeing my grand entrance, she froze mid-speech. Her microphone made an ear-splitting sound. Everyone winced. Embarrassed, I made my way to my best friends Lucia and Camila, who were waving and pointing to the seat they saved for me, one of the only open spots in the room. I tried to make myself small. But it was impossible. My roller coaster was now a huge, balloon-covered monstrosity.

Meli cleared her throat.

"Sorry, sorry," I said.

James and Janette, Meli's best friends, glared at me like a pair of mean bulldogs.

I finally plopped down between Lucia and Camila. They were on the flag football team too. "Did you like your surprise?" Lucia whispered, nudging me with her elbow.

"Loved it!" I whispered back.

"You're finally twelve," Camila squealed.

At the front of the cafetorium, Meli was talking again. "It's a condition that affects two percent of the popula—"

I tuned back out because Lucia added, "And Coach Street chose you for quarterback! He posted the team list on the athletics bulletin board first thing this morning."

"I can't believe it!" We fist-bumped. Then I realized the atmosphere had changed—the room was deadly quiet.

And Meli was completely silent on stage, giving me a hard, unblinking stare.

My heart thundered away. Oops, I guess we'd been talking too loudly. Meli glared at me like I was gum on the bottom of her shoe.

Mrs. Martinez, the strictest teacher in school, was looking at me too. "If we can't control ourselves, we'll be asked to leave," she announced. By "we" she meant "me."

Now *everyone* was staring.

James and Janette giggled.

Meli's eyes were focused straight ahead, her nostrils wide.

"Ooh, you're in trouble," Lucia sang under her breath beside me.

It wasn't my fault Dad got a flat tire and I was late. I didn't ask for all those huge balloons.

Plus, it was my *birthday*.

My pulse felt like waves crashing in my ears.

"I promise I'm done. You won't even know I'm here," I blurted, raising my hands in surrender. When the whole room gasped, I realized I'd forgotten I'd been holding the balloons.

Up, up, up they went.

For a second, I felt a thrill, like when you jump three checkers at once, or run a touchdown. *That'll show them*, the goblin said. Then Meli started blinking and her eyes glistened, and it was like I really was the gum on the bottom of someone's shoe.

The words ran out of my mouth all at once. "Sorry. So sorry, Meli! I can fix this." I climbed up onto one of the cafetorium tables to try to reach the balloon ribbons. The whole cafetorium started chanting, "Roxy! Roxy! Roxy!" as I gathered the balloons. Teachers ran up and down the rows of tables trying to shush everyone, but it was too late. Everyone was hyped up by the scene I'd caused. I wrapped the ribbons around my wrist and held them low and close to my chest. My cheeks were hot, and my heart was skipping every other beat.

"Go on," I said to Meli. But she only stood there in silence, looking at me so long without blinking I thought lasers were going to blast out of her eyeballs.

"You're the worst," Janette said under her breath, but everyone heard her. Lucia and Camila scowled in her direction. James scowled back at them.

My dad always says, "It's important to own up to your mistakes. Always. There's nothing worse than a person who can't admit when they're wrong."

I could hear him, like a tiny, Dad-shaped mouse in my ear, out-whispering the goblin.

The balloon ribbons still tight in my grip, I walked up to Meli.

"I'm sorry I ruined your presentation," I said. "It's super interesting and stuff. Please go on."

Meli's mouth had become a thin line. She was dressed like an artist. Paint brushes were tucked into the bun in her hair, and she was wearing a blue apron splattered with dried paint. Her hands were stuffed into the apron pockets. Meli breathed heavily and looked at my shoes like they were the most interesting thing in the world. Was she having a panic attack too? Because my heart was about to grow legs and run away from me.

"We good, Meli?" I asked in a whisper.

Slowly, Meli pulled a pair of shiny scissors out of her pocket. Then, in a quick motion of her arm, the scissors sliced through the ribbons, and the balloons rose into the rafters.

Everyone went bananas. Kids started hollering and whooping, Meli and I burst into tears, and Principal Salinas marched toward us shouting, "This assembly is *over*. Everyone else, back to their classes! Romero! Flores! To my office! NOW."

My balloons bobbed along the ceiling, ribbons trailing like long jellyfish tentacles. A few kids had managed to grab some, and they were leaving with them.

It was my birthday, and it was the last day of school, and everything was terrible.

CHAPTER 3
MELI

My whole life, I'd never been sent to the principal's office. I didn't even know what it looked like. I imagined the chairs had handcuffs and the windows were covered with bars to keep kids from escaping. Or worse, maybe Principal Salinas looked up all your grades and extra credit and made you watch on a giant touch screen as she swiped them clean forever.

We followed her down the empty hall. With each step, it felt like the sound of Principal Salinas's heels got louder and louder. Tap, tap, *bang*! Like a hammer.

Like all my plans for the summer were being nailed into a coffin. Deceased.

"This is a total nightmare," I said under my breath.

"At least it's not *your* birthday." Roxy crossed her arms but she looked shaken, with pieces of ribbon in her hair and her sad cardboard roller coaster sculpture flattened under her armpit.

"You don't get it. When Mami finds out, she'll call my dad in Spain. And what if he cancels—" But I couldn't say it out loud. All year long, Papi had been promising to take Benji and me to Legoland this summer if we got good grades and behaved. Now Roxy and her ridiculous balloons might've ruined everything.

"You two. Sit," Principal Salinas said, pointing a manicured finger at a couple of chairs outside her office door. "Wait here—quietly—while I call your parents."

I tucked my hands under my thighs. Beside me, Roxy picked at pieces of glitter on her box, staring at it like she was hypnotized.

"So much for my skit," she said.

"Yours? I'd barely started before you walked in looking like the house in Disney's *Up*."

"It's not my fault my friends got me balloons," she said, but all I heard was, *I can't help that I'm so popular.*

I decided to ignore her. Or at least I tried to. But the whole time we waited for our parents to arrive, she wouldn't stop breathing really loud. She rubbed her arms like she was cold, and I could see her hands were trembling. Then she started blinking. A lot.

"Are you okay?"

She was about to answer when Mrs. Esposito turned down the hallway, carrying my art project in a plastic crate. Whole clumps of it had come apart when someone, probably Roxy, knocked it over trying to catch a balloon. Mrs. Esposito placed it on my lap and smiled gently. "It was very brave what you shared, Melisa."

I could still feel my tears drying on my cheeks. Probably the whole school thought I was a crybaby. I didn't feel so brave now.

Roxy leaned toward me to look at the crate. "Cool sculpture."

"Shut up," I whispered.

"No, really, I mean it. But why a spine?"

It was a miniature spine made out of hundreds of seashells. I'd pasted them all together by hand and painted them bright blue. The spine was curved like an *S*, like the X-ray they'd taken of mine several months ago.

Begrudgingly, I said, "It's a representation of what's inside me. My spine, I mean. I have scoliosis." It felt weird telling her, but hadn't I been planning to tell the whole school? Now that she knew the truth, maybe Roxy would feel guilty about spoiling my presentation. At least I hoped she would.

Instead she looked like a flashbulb had gone off inside her head. "Oh, is that the thing they checked us for at the beginning of the year? When we all had to touch our toes in front of the nurse?"

I nodded and held up a blue conch. After rehearsing my lines for weeks, I still wanted someone, anyone, to hear them. Even if it was just Roxy. "The shells represent my bones. I picked them at the beach specifically for their imperfections. They all have holes or chips." That's how I'd felt the day the doctors confirmed my diagnosis. Like I wasn't the same shape as everyone else. *All of us are unique and different*, Mami had said, but she didn't know what it was like to be a sixth grader. Everyone wants to be unique. Nobody wants to be different.

"But they're still beautiful," Roxy said.

"Exactly." I hadn't expected her, of all people, to get it. It'd taken me weeks to figure out all the emotions I had about my scoliosis, and creating the sculpture was a big part of that. "Still beautiful," I echoed.

"My roller coaster was supposed to represent something, too, you know."

I tried to imagine what. It looked like she'd just taken one of the boxes Mami had used to pack up my room and splattered it with paint and glitter, but I didn't say so.

Before Roxy could explain any further, our parents arrived. They barged through the school entrance, rushing down the hallway and holding hands the entire time.

Mami looked down and met my eyes. "Oh, Meli. I expected better from you."

The tears I'd cried in the cafetorium were resurfacing, stinging underneath my eyelids.

"What happened, kiddo?" From Carlos's worried, soft tone, you'd think Roxy had fallen off the stage and broken a leg instead of destroying *my* sculpture. She lowered her head and he reached for her hand, squeezing it just once. It was like they had a secret language.

I crossed my arms because I could already see where this was going: Mami would make sure I learned my lesson, Carlos would go easy on Roxy, and Roxy would keep getting away with things, forever and ever.

Principal Salinas opened the door and gestured for us to come into her office. "Mr. Romero. Ms. Flores. I'm sorry to pull you out of work like this."

Mami and Carlos exchanged worried glances. I hadn't noticed until now that they weren't in their work clothes. Mami wore a faded old T-shirt and yoga pants, and Carlos's jeans were all torn up and splattered with paint. It wasn't like my mom at all. She was a manager at a doctor's office (basically a professional organizer) and she liked everything to be clean and in order, always. But now the only non-scruffy thing about her was the shiny new engagement ring on her finger. I wished it would fall in wet cement.

"Well, it's a good thing we'd taken the day off to work on the new house," Mami said, glaring straight at me. "We were very upset to hear the girls were fighting."

"*Fighting*'s a strong word, right, buds?" Carlos waved one hand like he was clearing the air between me and Roxy. But neither one of us answered his question. Who did Carlos think he was calling *buds*? There was no way he was this nice. He reminded me of those parents Mami always said tried too hard to be their kids' best friends. *I'm your parent first,* she loved to remind me.

Which was fine because I didn't need any more pals. Especially not Roxy and her Muppet dad.

He cleared his throat awkwardly. "Would you call it fighting, Principal Salinas?"

"I'd call it inciting chaos on the last day of school." She looked frazzled, like she'd just run a marathon. "In any case, I can't give them detention like we normally would. The best I can do is early dismissal."

For half a second, I was excited, until I realized what that really meant. "But I was supposed to have lunch with James and Janette and the rest of the art club today. Ms. Ledero is getting us pizza and ice cream!"

Roxy nearly jumped out of her chair. "And I haven't even said goodbye to all my friends! Coach Street said we were going to play noodle hockey for our last PE class!"

Principal Salinas shook her head and stood up. "I'm sorry, girls. You'll just have to go home. Do not pass go. Do not collect two hundred dollars."

"What?" Roxy looked flabbergasted. Our parents twisted their lips like they didn't know to smile or frown.

"It's a Monopoly reference," I said, rolling my eyes. Principal Salinas was always acting like punishing kids was funny to her.

"I know what it is," Roxy snapped. "It's just a major upset."

"Bueno, home it is." Mami gathered her purse and handed me my backpack.

"Can we go to our *actual* home?" Roxy asked. "Not the new—"

"Roxana Romero. Think before you make this worse," Carlos said. His voice was so stern, it even scared me a little. I slipped my hand into Mami's.

She sighed. "Maybe now that it's summer you'll both make an effort to work together instead of against each other," Mami added.

Principal Salinas walked us toward the door. "Do the girls have a history of clashing?"

Carlos shook his head. "No, not at all. Well . . . there was a thing at the restaurant the other night. But those were just end-of-the-year jitters, right, girls?"

I looked down at my shoes, thinking about the restaurant and the broken dishes, and Carlos and Mami announcing their engagement on an iPad like it was no big deal. *Surprise! Life as you know it is over and you have to live with Roxy now! Next slide, please.*

I wished things could be like they used to be with me and Mami. She could fix anything, and if I had a fight with James or Janette, or a crush on somebody in my class, she always gave the best advice. Now that Carlos was in the picture, suddenly she wanted his help and his opinions on everything. So there was no way I could tell Mami what I really thought about Roxy without getting in big trouble.

If I were honest, if I said that Roxy just . . . me cae mal—like when you eat something that doesn't agree with you—then I might as well have said goodbye to Legoland, and going to art camp with James and Janette, and basically having any fun at all this summer.

"I just had a stomachache. Something didn't agree with me." But I couldn't help looking right at Roxy as I said it.

Her eyes grew wide, like she knew I meant her. "Yeah, and I have a pain in the bu—"

"But we're better, now," I interrupted, afraid Roxy's mouth would only make our parents get even more upset at us.

Mami and Carlos sighed in relief and smiled at each other, but Roxy looked furious that I'd cut her off.

Good. I picked up the crate with my sculpture in it. Maybe now she'd know how it felt to be talked over. To have your voice drowned out by someone else's. To be made to feel invisible.

"You'll see," Carlos said. "We're going to have a great summer."

I walked ahead of him so I wouldn't have to pretend to smile. *Have a great summer* was what Roxy had written in my yearbook last year right before she took my purple pen. It's what popular kids wrote to kids they didn't like, or to kids they didn't know existed.

The Romeros' words were empty, now more than ever.

CHAPTER 4
ROXY

"Tu celulár, Melisa," Evy said in the school parking lot. Meli dug into her bag and handed over her cell phone.

I put my hand in my pocket, ready to give up my phone too.

But Dad was about as uncomfortable punishing Ben and me as a kid wearing a tuxedo at the beach. "It's been a stressful time, Evy."

Meli's mouth fell open and her eyes darted from Dad to her mom. Then she locked eyes on me. She had a look on her face that said, "I'd drop a house on you if I could."

"If the girls agree to let bygones be bygones—" Dad started to say.

"—then I suppose we can let them off the hook," Evy finished. She held Meli's phone up, adding, "Pero se portan bien from now on, okay?"

"We will!" Meli said, taking her phone back before her mom could change her mind.

I looked at Dad, and it was like we were in our own private huddle for a moment. I mouthed the word *thanks*.

But what they did next was nearly as bad as losing every privilege we had for a week.

After signing the Bens out of school early too—Meli and I stood side by side in chilly silence while the adults filled out the early dismissal form—they brought us all to the new house, where Dad and Evy had hung a HAPPY BIRTHDAY sign over the front door.

"It's a little earlier than we expected, but . . . welcome home, kids!" Dad and Evy said together. Inside, colorful balloons were tied to the furniture.

I nudged Meli sharply with an elbow. "You didn't bring your scissors, did you?"

"I wish," she grumbled. Evy, Meli, and Benji had moved in the day before and their stuff was in boxes everywhere. I spotted some of my stuff in boxes too. Dad had been moving our possessions in slowly. Meli nudged a box labeled ROXY'S TOYS.

"Those aren't toys, by the way," I said.

Meli smirked. "It says *toys*."

"It's a box of sports equipment. Footballs and cleats and stuff. You wouldn't know about that." I got up and tried to push the box away. But then the lid popped open, revealing my Baby Sleeps-a-Lot doll, her hair all matted and wild. Mom had given her to me when I was a baby.

The goblin shouted, *You are so embarrassing, Roxy.*

Meli's eyebrows went up, but she didn't say a word.

Why couldn't we be more like the Bens? My brother had immediately gone out to explore the backyard, a book tucked under his arm. As usual, Benji followed. "Hold up, Bro!" he'd called, karate chopping the air. I don't know how they did it—Ben was always so quiet, his nose planted in a book, while Benji was like a remote-control car, always zipping around and bumping into things. Benji was smaller than Ben, who was tall for his age. They both loved dinosaurs but disagreed on which ones were cooler. Even so, they got along like peanut butter and jelly.

Meanwhile, Meli and I sat on a pair of folding chairs in the living room, as still as statues, ignoring each other.

In the kitchen, our parents whispered as they worked, and I could just imagine what they were saying.

Ay, Dios mío, these girls just can't get along.

Let's figure out a way to torture them further!

I know! We can send them away to boarding school. Forever!

I watched as Dad and Evy talked quietly. From time to time, he'd touch her hair, and she'd lean into him. As far as I knew, Dad hadn't had any girlfriends after breaking up with Mom. It was strange to see him this way with someone. Suddenly, Evy looked in my direction and our eyes locked. Then she winked and kept on chatting with Dad. That set my brain off again.

I could just guess what Evy was thinking. *"Boy, Roxy sure is nosy!"*

My imagination may have been running away from me, but with every passing hour of my birthday, things seemed to get worse. As for Meli, she was staring at the carpet, which was matted and sickly green, like someone had mashed up an avocado and left it out for too long.

"So," I started. "This is our new house. It's a total fixer-upper."

Meli nodded without looking up. "More fixer, less upper, I'd say." Meli pulled her phone from her pocket and started scrolling.

I looked around. My mom would have adored the place. Back when she still lived in Miami, before the depression got worse and made her go live with Abuelo, she was always redecorating. She joked that color had an expiration date in her house. One day, the kitchen would be pink. The next time Ben and I came over, it would be blue.

I closed my eyes and imagined Mom walking through the house. I pictured her on a good day when she wasn't depressed and was her usual, lively self. "Mira, Roxy," she would say, pointing at the molding that wrapped around the room. "Let's paint it with polka dots!" I imagined her sneaking up behind me and giving my neck a little massage, like she sometimes did. I almost felt her kissing the top of my head.

Meli giggled at something on her phone. She was probably texting James and Janette, telling them all about me and the box of toys. Or something like that.

Shh, I told the goblin.

I pulled out my phone, too, and stared at the screen. Suddenly a notification popped up. Meli was sharing her contact information with me.

"Oh," I said. "Thanks."

"Send me yours?"

"Sure," I agreed, and quickly did.

We sat in silence for a bit longer. Then my phone pinged an alert.

"Wanna see what the rest of the house looks like?" Meli had texted.

"Yup!" I texted back, laughing to myself. Maybe we would actually get along better this way. No real contact. Just texts.

Meli stood up and I followed her. We left the living room, which had a real fireplace, all dirty from soot. The old owners must have loved sweating. I didn't know anyone in Florida with a fireplace! "There are three rooms upstairs and a big bedroom downstairs," Meli said. "Benji and I slept with Mami in the big room last night."

We climbed the stairs and walked into another room with windows that looked out on the pool and trampoline.

"A pool. We have a pool. That's lucky."

Meli sat cross-legged on the carpet. "Doesn't feel lucky. I liked my old house."

"And I like mine. It's colorful and messy and Lucia and Camila live around the corner."

"James and Janette live down the block from my old house."

"Bummer," I said sarcastically, thinking of the way James and Janette glared at me earlier.

Meli's mouth dropped open and she took a big breath, like she was about to tell me off, then reconsidered.

We looked around the top floor some more. Surprisingly, the carpet was new. Meli sighed. "At least we'll have our own rooms upstairs. In my old house, I had to share with Benji." She made a puke face, and I did, too. Sharing a room sounded like a nightmare.

"Our own rooms. I guess that's not so bad."

Meli narrowed her eyes. "Are you trying to look on the bright side now, Roxana Romero?"

My heart picked up speed. Was Meli just joking? Or was she poking fun? I could never tell with her. Why couldn't we just understand each other? If she was joking, I would joke, too. I forced a laugh, then said, "My mistake."

But Meli didn't smile. I took my time in the hallway, peering into the empty rooms, and wondered about the family that used to live here. Were they happy? Something told me they had been. Dad always said houses had "vibrations," and that if you concentrated hard, you could feel whether the vibrations were good or bad. My old house definitely had good vibrations, even though Mom and Dad had broken up long ago. Dad once explained that he and Mom had married very young and that they had grown apart. Mom said, "Sometimes people want different things out of life." Even though they weren't married to each other, I knew that Mom and Dad still loved each other in their own, separate ways. Their divorce had happened so long ago that I didn't have any clear memories of when they were together. It had always been this way, or so it seemed to me. In fact, I couldn't picture Dad with anyone. A two-parent family just felt . . . weird.

The next thing I knew, Evy was shouting, "¡Carlos, corre!"

Meli and I ran out in time to see the Bens both pointing at the kitchen at the same time. Water was spouting from the sink like a fountain and spraying everywhere.

Dad flew past us like he had the ball and was running for the end zone. The stream was trickling out of the kitchen, soaking the green carpet and forming puddles at our feet.

Dad and Evy started yelling in the kitchen. "Turn off the valve!" Dad said.

Evy was under the sink, her legs sticking out. "I am! The water keeps coming," Evy shouted.

"Clockwise! Turn it clockwise!" Dad shouted.

"What does it look like I'm doing?" Evy yelled back.

"Turn it to the right! Lefty loosey, righty tighty!" Dad insisted.

Benji had somehow found and unpacked his water blasters and both boys had filled them up and started a water fight in the hall.

"If they come near me with those things I'm going to drown them," I said.

"And I'll help," Meli added.

Finally Dad and Evy gave up on stopping the leak. "Lift as many boxes as you can off the floor!" Dad said, and we all went to work, putting up everything that we could. The water wouldn't stop gushing from the pipe in the kitchen. It poured through the house like a river, and soon, we were ankle-deep in cold water.

Dad called an emergency plumber, who took one look at the busted pipe, sucked his teeth, and called it one of the worst situations he'd ever seen.

Meli's mom sloshed into the living room. She was drenched and her makeup was running down her face. "Meli, pack a bag of dry clothes and your toothbrush. We can spend the night at Carlos's house. Don't forget your brace."

Excuse me? This was putting la tapa on el pomo. The last straw. The breaking point.

Not only was my birthday ruined and my sneakers soaked, but now the night had morphed into a sleepover with the last person on earth I wanted to spend time with.

Meli wasn't thrilled about the arrangement either. "What? No! Can I just stay at Janette's?"

Evy raised one eyebrow slowly, like somebody was pulling it with a string. Meli stomped her foot and water splashed up her leg, but she didn't say anything else.

The plumber managed to shut off the water, but he said he wouldn't be back until the next day. "This is a big job. A very big job. You got insurance, right?"

"We do," Dad said.

Outside, Meli and Benji were in their mom's car, and Ben and I loaded into Dad's van. Dad went over to Evy's car and gave her another kiss. Sheesh. "It's going to be okay, Evy. Ya verás."

She nodded and kissed him back.

Meli was in the front seat of her mom's car, making a gagging gesture at the sight of our parents kissing. The two of us didn't agree on much, but I was with her on this one.

As Dad backed out of the driveway, Meli texted me:

This has been the longest day.

I wrote back:

Yep. The worst and longest. A complete disasterpiece.

We dragged ourselves into my house looking like we'd been caught in a bad storm. We all changed into dry clothes. Dad called us into the living room, where he'd laid an old comforter down on the floor. "Picnic dinner!" he announced. Ben sat down on the comforter right away, and Benji joined him.

"What's this?" Meli asked.

I sighed. "Picnic dinner is something my mom made whenever one of us was feeling down. Dad kept it up. It's just dinner in the living room, sitting on the floor. It used to be, I don't know, it was . . . special back then."

Slowly I made my way to the comforter and sat with my knees drawn up. Meli sat beside me. Dad gave us each a sandwich, a bag of cheese puffs, and a juice pouch. We'd left my birthday meal of build-your-own-tacos at the fixer-upper.

"Watch out for picnic-thieving ants!" Dad joked before sitting down too. Evy joined us last. She sat down slowly, unsure of what to do with her plate. I watched as she picked up a piece of lint off the carpet and made a face.

Ben and Benji started a game right away, trying to toss cheese puffs into each other's mouths. "Oigan," Evy said, "don't make a mess."

"It's nothing a vacuum can't pick up," Dad said, and tossed a cheese puff at Benji. It bounced off his nose. Evy sighed and kept eating her sandwich. Her jaw muscles flexed impressively as she ate. Meli nudged me with an elbow and pointed her chin at her mother in a did-you-catch-that gesture.

I caught it, all right.

"You know," I said, "we have picnic dinners all the time." I chewed and spoke with a mouthful of ham sandwich. I shoved a cheese puff in, too, then wiped my fingers on the comforter.

"Really?" Benji asked excited. "We can't even bring a single potato chip out of the kitchen or Mami makes this face." He scrunched up his nose and puckered his mouth.

Evy laughed, but I could tell Benji's imitation got under her skin. "Don't exaggerate now," she said softly.

"He isn't," Meli piped up. "Mami can see a crumb from a mile away. Like an eagle."

"Or a pterodactyl!" Benji added, then he screeched at the top of his lungs.

"Now, now," Dad began. "We could all be a little neater around here." He gave me a warning look, so I ate the rest of my sandwich in silence. In fact, everyone got a little quiet, and I figured that we were all doing a whole lot of thinking.

Afterward, Meli and I went to my room and we set up the inflatable mattress for her. "Is that your mom?" Meli asked, pointing at the framed photo on my nightstand. "She has freckles like you." In the picture, Mom had her hair in a ponytail and was wearing overalls. She was on the highest rung of a ladder, painting our house purple. We lived in the only lavender-colored house in our neighborhood. All the other homes were painted some version of boring white—beige, taupe, even French vanilla. Back when I was just a baby, Mom had insisted on the perfect shade of purple for our home. In the mornings, the color was a stormy kind of gray, but in the afternoons, the house was all lilac and glowing. I only know the details because Dad took that photograph of her while she worked, and he told me the story.

"Yeah. That's her a long time ago."

Meli looked around. My room was purple, too, but my ceiling was blue. Mom had painted a bright white crescent moon in one corner of the ceiling, and she'd dotted the rest of the "sky" with stars. She used to call me her *cielito lindo*.

"She painted your whole house, didn't she?" Meli asked.

I nodded, then wiped my eyes with the inside of my shirt. Leaving this house would mean leaving mom's art behind. It meant leaving my cielito lindo. Someone had made "a good offer" on our house and Dad had taken it. He'd just taken it, without asking me or Ben. How was that fair? Meanwhile, Mom was a million miles away with Abuelo, and she hadn't even taken her art supplies. These days she hardly ever came to the phone when I called. "She's getting stronger every day," Abuelo assured me. I glanced up at the ceiling again. Those stars seemed like all I had left of her, and soon, somebody else was going to own them and paint over them, make it so that they never existed.

"It's very beautiful," Meli said.

"Thanks. I'm sure your old house was great too."

Meli shrugged. "It was okay. The main thing is it was ours. Mine, Mami's, Benji's, and Papi's, at least until he moved out. It's the last place we were all a family. And now Mami thinks we can just form a new family, like that." Meli snapped her fingers. "Now I don't know what it means to be a Flores anymore." Meli sniffed, but I didn't look her way in case she was crying too. I never wanted anybody to look at me when I cried.

I sat quietly for a bit, trying to snap my fingers too. I was never able to make a sound, and it always frustrated me. When I looked up, Meli was staring at me. Did she think I was making fun? I sat on my hands quickly.

"We can't let them do this to us," Meli said after a while. "We have to convince them this is a mistake."

I flipped on my side to face her. The mattress squeaked. "You're right. Families don't just come together like that," I said, attempting another silent finger snap.

"Ha ha," Meli said sarcastically.

I shrugged. Sometimes, it was too hard to explain yourself. And with Meli, it felt like I was explaining myself all the time.

"Maybe you don't care, but . . . ," she said after a while.

"I do care. A lot." My face felt hot, and my muscles tensed up, like they sometimes did on the field when the other team said nasty things under their breath. I inhaled deeply before talking. "What if we don't try to convince them with words? What if we *show* them what a mistake this would all be?"

Meli's eyes widened, an idea clearly forming in her mind. I could almost picture a tiny lightbulb turning on over her head like in a cartoon. "You're right. The proof that we are incompatible as a family is right in front of our faces. I mean, first, the Romeros are slobs!"

"Hey!"

"Be honest. I have eyeballs, you know." Meli

stared pointedly at a pile of dirty socks in the corner of my room, then turned her eyes to the three empty cups on my dresser.

"Okay," I admitted. "Our laundry piles up, and the backyard is always full of leaves and weeds, and Ben's feet stink."

Meli cracked a smile, then got serious again.

"What about you? Evy is a total Cleanzilla." I curled my hands into claws. "Rawr! Vacuum everything or I'll—" I stopped myself.

"Go on," Meli said, steely voiced, her eyes narrowed at me.

"Or I'll clean it myself!" I said in a Godzilla growl.

Meli just about smiled again but stopped short. "You're right, Roxy. Mami would lose it if she had to pick up after you guys. She's super neat and obsessed with cleaning. And we have to eat healthy too. Did you catch her side-eyeing the cheese puffs? I haven't had junk food in ages."

"This is perfect!" I said, sitting up on my knees. "Keep going! Dad hates perfume. It stuffs up his nose so he can't breathe, and he sounds funny."

"Like a Muppet?" Meli asked, her face looking like it was about to explode into laughter.

"I mean, I guess," I said.

Meli howled with laughter. "He's exactly like a Muppet!"

That one hurt. Sure, Dad was sometimes clumsy and liked to crack jokes, and maybe his hair could use a good combing now and then, but didn't Meli see how gentle he was? And how fun?

I must have been making a face because Meli said, "Sorry. I just meant he's goofy, in a fun way." She rolled off the air mattress and sat on mine. "My mom absolutely hates it when we walk in the house with shoes on."

I reached down and grabbed my sneakers. "I will wear these to bed if I have to!"

"You'd better. And she hates scary movies. She watched one as a kid about a little girl who gets sucked into a television and she never recovered."

"Are you kidding me? Dad loves Halloween! We

even make a haunted house for the neighbors to go through every year. You should see the terrifying props we have in the attic!"

"What else?" Meli urged.

"Dad hates it when anybody opens a window or leaves a door ajar. He starts shouting about the A/C escaping the house."

"And Mami loves fresh air!" Meli was nodding now.

"Dad watches chess videos online. Chess. Videos," I pretended to snore loudly and Meli cracked up.

"Mami is obsessed with telenovelas. So much drama!"

"Dad hates vegetables shaped like trees."

"Like broccoli and cauliflower? They're Mami's favorites!" Meli crossed her arms. "No offense, but your dad doesn't seem like soulmate material for my mom."

I picked up the picture frame on my nightstand. The way Mom looked at Dad was like he was the whole solar system. He must have stared at her too like she was the sun itself.

"My dad already had a soulmate," I said.

Meli nodded. "The two of us are clearly disasters together, which means they probably will be too. Maybe we can convince them that this"—Meli paused to gesture at everything around us, encompassing the new house, our parents, their pasts, and futures—"is a mistake."

"Us. Sisters. What were they even thinking?"

We both grew quiet.

There was a knock on the door, then it opened. It was Evy. She was holding a plastic contraption dotted with pink stars. It had Velcro straps that curled and dangled. "Tu brace, mi niña," Evy said, holding the brace out for Meli.

"Can't we skip it tonight?"

Evy shook her head. "You know it's important. Póntelo."

I watched as Evy helped Meli slip the brace around her body. Meli was almost as tall as her mom. It felt like I was watching something private, so I closed my eyes. I heard the crackle of the Velcro and Meli made a sound like *oof*.

"Good night, girls," I heard Evy say, and when I opened my eyes again, Meli was back in bed with her blanket up to her neck. Evy closed the door.

"Stop staring," Meli said.

"I wasn't looking, I swear."

"It's just a nighttime thing, you know. Some kids have to wear it all day. But if we can stop the curve while I grow, then I won't need surgery," Meli whispered.

"You're already taller than me by a lot!"

"That's the point. My papi is really tall. *Much* taller than Carlos, so I'm probably going to keep growing."

I ignored her comment about how tall my dad was compared to hers. It was true—Dad and Evy were the same height. "You know," I said, "if you ever do have to wear the brace to school, and someone tries to punch you in the gut, they'd be in for a surprise."

Meli chuckled. "My doctor calls it my superhero armor."

"There you go," I said. "Does it . . . hurt?"

"No. But it's not exactly comfortable."

"Do you—"

"You can stop asking questions now."

I was just curious. Meli didn't have to be bossy about it.

Yeah, shut up already, went the goblin.

Meli (and the goblin) were right. I didn't mean to be nosy. It's not like I wanted Meli asking me a ton of questions about the anxiety I sometimes felt.

After a while Meli spoke again, as if we hadn't been interrupted by her mom with the brace. "Sisters. Hmph. Can you imagine? Never."

"Never ever," I agreed.

"Tomorrow, we make a plan to show our parents that they DO NOT belong together."

"Our master plan. It has to work," I said.

"Not a master plan. A *disaster* plan. And it *will* work. I know it," Meli said. She adjusted a strap on her brace, then lay down. "Good night, Roxy."

The overhead lights were still on. I grabbed one of my sneakers and chucked it at the switch on the wall. Bull's-eye! The room went dark.

"I bet that left a mark," I said.

"Oh my gosh, my mom is going to hate that so much," Meli said.

"Good." We were quiet then, both of us lost in thought. I couldn't wait until all this was over and Meli, her mom, and her brother were out of my life forever. Meli was probably thinking the same thing about me, Dad, and Ben.

I turned it all over in my mind for a long time before going to sleep, and when I finally did, I dreamed of Godzilla carrying a toilet brush.

Part Two:

The ~~Master~~ Disaster Plan

CHAPTER 5
MELI

If someone had told me that by the start of the summer before seventh grade I'd be sleeping over at Roxy's, Mami would be engaged to her dad, and we'd have a new house that was underwater, I wouldn't have believed it. In a blink Mami had gone and made all these big decisions without us, and now nothing was in my control. Was this how the rest of the summer would be? The rest of my whole life? I stirred, still half asleep, wishing I could pop this air mattress, and poof! Life would go back to normal. But instead, a familiar roaring snapped me back to reality.

"What is that?!" Roxy said.

The high-pitched motor sound traveled through the halls. It could only mean one thing. "Mami's cleaning. You've never heard the sound of a vacuum before?"

"Not at this hour!" She flipped her pillow over her head. Since she wasn't looking, I took the chance to take off my night brace under the covers. The plastic was hard like a helmet, and the Velcro keeping it tight around my back screeched louder than I expected.

"And what was that?!" Roxy groaned again.

"Shhhh!! If she hears we're awake, she'll recruit us to start cleaning too!" As quietly as I could, I stretched into a few cat-cows and child's poses. The brace always left my back feeling stiff and a little sore, but I didn't see why I had to explain any of this to Roxy. She was Miss Sporty MVP and Captain of Everything—she wouldn't understand what it's like to have doctors checking on you all the time, or giving you exercises to do at home. It was scary sometimes. I knew that yoga and my brace were good for me. My doctor had said that if I stayed on top of both, there was a possibility I wouldn't need surgery. But every once in a while, all I could think was, *What if it doesn't work? What if I just get worse?*

I tilted my head back and took a deep breath. To my complete surprise, Roxy slowly got on her hands and knees and started mirroring me. "What are you doing?" I hissed. Was she making fun of me? "It looks cool," she whispered. "Show me more. Coach Street's always saying we should stretch."

I pretended to ignore her and got into a downward dog. It was my favorite pose because whenever I bent my body into an A shape, the world turned upside down in a good way. Roxy followed my lead, wobbling as if her arms were spaghetti.

"That's not funny. Just hold still and keep quiet," I said as the sound of the vacuum got closer, then faded. Now we were frozen on all fours with our butts in the air.

"You know, some people use alarm clocks," Roxy whispered. Her cheeks looked weird upside down and her face was getting red from all the blood rushing to her head.

I muffled a giggle. Roxy's sense of humor always reminded me of something Papi used to say, that every joke has an ounce of truth in it. Last night she'd called Mami a Cleanzilla, and now that I was literally looking at things from a new perspective, I wondered if she actually thought Mami was a monster. That was mean, wasn't it? Mami could be a little strict but she meant well, and maybe her rules were there for a reason. Before she'd met Carlos, *our* house had never flooded from one chaotic moment to another. I wished Roxy wouldn't write Mami off just because she wasn't perfect.

But then again, I wished Carlos *would*.

I nearly lost my balance as the first idea for our Disaster Plan hit me like a boomerang. "Wait a minute. Is your dad also not a morning person like you?"

"Pfft." Roxy let out the biggest yawn I'd ever seen. "He's the least morning person I know. He makes owls look like early birds."

"This is perfect." I stood and started gathering my clothes. "The sooner we get up, the grumpier he'll be. Just imagine our first day living together and he'll be in the worst mood ever."

Roxy crawled back into her bed. "I bet my dad's worst mood ever isn't nearly as bad as your—"

"My what?" I snapped.

"Nothing. I was just agreeing with you, sheesh. Can't I sleep five more minutes?"

"We can't waste any time! If you're annoyed, imagine your dad multiplied by ten."

"It's too early for math, Meli."

I tossed a plush alien at her and darted to the bathroom to get dressed. In my best impersonation of Mami, I yelled, "¡Es un nuevo dia, Roxy! Time for a clean start."

It seemed we weren't the only ones who wished the vacuum cleaner had a snooze button. The boys were slouched over the kitchen island; Ben was trying to read the back of the cereal box while Benji picked the raisins out of his bowl one by one. Carlos was still in his pj's, pushing the buttons on the coffee maker like it was a video game controller that had run out of batteries.

I nudged Roxy with my elbow and raised my eyebrows toward her dad. She was still half asleep, too, but she immediately got the message.

"Here, Dad, let me do it!" she said, reaching for a seafoam-green mug.

Carlos exhaled and kissed her on the forehead. "My kid, the heroine," he said, not noticing that as soon as he turned around, Roxy grabbed a decaf K-Cup. We exchanged tiny nods as she plopped it in and the machine began to pour.

While we waited for *that* mini mischief to develop, I offered to help Mami make breakfast.

"You're the best, Meli. There's a fresh tub of yogurt in the fridge. Oh, and I bought strawberries, blueberries, and raspberries too."

"When did you go to the grocery store?" Carlos asked.

"This morning. While you were sleeping," Mami said. Then she took out her phone, started streaming her favorite reggaeton mix on the Bluetooth speaker, and slipped her hands into a pair of yellow rubber gloves.

"Uh-oh. Now the gloves have come *on*," I said to Roxy.

She signaled for me to follow her into their walk-in pantry. It was like being in the cereal and cookie aisle at Publix. There were boxes in every color, everywhere.

"What's with the yellow gloves?" she asked.

"It's basically mom code for 'I'm about to make everything spotless.'"

"Excellent. Watch this." She took a bottle of pancake syrup off the shelf and plopped it in front of the Benjamins. "We usually have waffles on weekends, not yogurt. Right, Ben?"

"Yeah! With chocolate chips!"

"Oh. I guess that's all right." Mami's eyes were fixated on the bottle. It wasn't even the real, natural stuff. The cap had bits of dried syrup sticking out from the edges. She wiped it down with a damp paper towel and said, "We'll just top the waffles with fruit."

Right, the fruit! That was my cue. I opened the fridge and took out the berries, stacking one plastic container on top of the other. But when I went to close the door—

"Oops!" An avalanche of fruit fell all over the freshly vacuumed floor.

Without missing a beat, Roxy sprang into action. "I'll help clean it up!" For every two berries she picked up, she stepped on a bunch more.

"¡Roxy, espera!" Mami said.

But she'd already left juicy blue-and-red track marks all over the kitchen. "Are those from my shoes?"

I had to bite my lip to keep from laughing. All these years I'd thought Roxy was just another athlete, but turns out she was a pretty decent actress. While Mami told her to take her shoes off so she could clean them, Roxy made a big deal of apologizing and looked like she felt really bad about the whole thing. It was an inspired performance. So good, in fact, that her dad came over to rub her back. Carlos to her rescue, like always.

"It's okay, Rox, these things happen." But Mami's

forehead had started to crinkle, and she'd gotten real quiet. "Right, Evy?" Carlos added.

"Hmm? Oh, right. But let's leave our shoes outside from now on, okay?"

I tried to think fast as Carlos took a sip of his decoy decaf. Mami had set her trusty cleaning supply bucket on one of the barstools, so I went through it and grabbed the strongest-smelling spray I could find.

"Here, I'll clean up!" I started misting the floor with Fabuloso but sprayed Carlos by "accident."

"Meli, no!"

"Evy, it's okay," Carlos said. "Tranquila."

Mami's left eyebrow shot up, quick as a rocket ship. She *hated* being told to calm down.

"The girls are just excited to be—wait." He sniffed at his sleeve and coughed. "Is that lavender?"

I looked down at the ingredients label on the bottle. "It just says 'fragrance.'"

"That's not good." Carlos's voice sounded like someone had plugged his nostrils shut. His eyes were starting to get watery too.

Mami ran to the bathroom and came back with

two handfuls of tissue. "Here, take these. I'll open some windows."

"Don't! You'll let out all the A/C!" Carlos yelled.

"Oye. Tranquilo," Mami said, throwing back what Carlos had just told her seconds ago. "How else are we supposed to get the smell out?"

"It's wasteful."

"It's a few minutes!"

It was all coming together more beautifully than we could have imagined. Roxy and I sat next to the Benjamins on the kitchen island and tried not to smile as our parents' voices grew louder and their words faster.

"It's just air. Don't worry so much," Mami said.

"Me? You're the one cleaning at the crack of dawn!"

Benji and I gasped. That was a huge mistake on Carlos's part. I checked the time on the microwave oven. It was official—this whole engagement would be toast within minutes.

"This makes me wish we had popcorn," I whispered.

"Here." Roxy passed me the bag of chocolate chips. "Even better."

"Are you saying you don't care if the house is a pigsty?" Mami said. She took off her gloves and slapped them against the sink. Carlos placed his hands on her shoulders and pressed his forehead against hers.

"Vida. The house is not that bad. And none of this will matter once we're at the new house. *Our* new house. Together."

They took a deep breath in sync.

Oh no.

Then they smiled and kissed.

Ew.

"You're right," Mami said. "We just need to focus on the positive."

"Exactly," Carlos said. He wrapped his arm around her and gestured at us and the Benjamins. "Like the fact that we get to start fixing up the house today!"

My little brother's eyes lit up. "Does this mean we get to knock things down with giant hammers?"

"Not quite," Carlos said. "But since you girls seem

so eager to lend a hand this morning, how about we take all that energy over to the new place?"

"Oh. Sounds fun, Dad," Roxy said, but when she looked at me, her eyes were screaming: *What now?!*

I smiled as our parents started making a list of everything we'd need from the home improvement store. Sure, our Disaster Plan was off to a rough start, but I had a feeling it'd all come together in the new house. The fixer-upper had plenty of chaos to go around.

CHAPTER 6
ROXY

Was Meli Flores still the most annoying person I knew?

Yes.

Was I totally impressed by her absolutely bananas behavior at the home improvement store?

Absolutely yes! Right off the bat, Meli managed to spill a box of nails. "Oops!" she said as the nails clattered to the floor, rolling under the shelves. Ben and Benji started kicking them around, but my dad made the boys stop, then he picked them both up and plopped them into the shopping cart. Ben's legs were too long for it, but he curled up like a doodlebug and made room for Benji, who was smaller.

They were squeezed together in there, but at least they were contained.

"Clean up on aisle five!" we heard over the speaker.

"Ay, que vergüenza," Evy moaned, her cheeks turning red.

"Sorry!" Meli said.

"Accidents happen," Dad said, then broke into a huge yawn. "I need another cup of coffee. The last one did nothing for me. I don't have any energy today."

Meli looked my way, gave me a wink, then mouthed, *Your turn.*

Up and down the aisles we went while I wracked my brain to come up with another way to disrupt the lovefest going on between my dad and Evy. She had looped her arm with his as he pushed the shopping cart. I was getting used to the way they always stood close together, touching. A bubble of guilt formed in my throat, but I popped it with one big swallow.

Whenever Evy pointed at something, like a patio set or a light fixture, Dad would say, "You have such good taste!"

Gross.

Evy went and got a second shopping cart, and soon it was full of supplies—paint cans, caulking tools, air filters, ceiling fans, and lightbulbs. The stuff formed a tower in the cart. We headed out into the garden section.

Dad picked up a pink hibiscus flower from the ground. Gently, he tucked it behind Evy's ear and she actually blushed, like a princess in a movie meeting her prince for the first time. I couldn't take it!

"Do something!" Meli whispered, but I couldn't seem to make a choice. Should I pick a fight with the boys? That would just get me grounded. "Come on!" Meli urged.

"Like what?" I shot back at her. Meli was being *super* pushy.

Finally she narrowed her eyes at me, then ran ahead. She fell to the ground, crying. "My toe! My toe! Carlos ran over my toe with the shopping cart!"

Dad stopped in his tracks. "I did? Oh no, Meli. I'm so sorry!"

Evy sat on the floor and yanked off Meli's pink

boots and mismatched socks. "Let me see. Can you wiggle it?"

Meli cried out and said she couldn't. Beside me, Dad's face went pale.

Oh, she was good. Maybe too good.

"We can go to the urgent care clinic and get an X-ray and check your back, too, in case you hurt it when you fell," Evy told Meli. My heart raced. A doctor would know right away that she wasn't hurt at all! I locked eyes with Meli and shook my head hard. Abort mission!

"I think I can move it after all," Meli said, wiggling her toes. "Just a bruise, I guess. It feels better already."

Dad released a big breath. "Thank goodness!" he said, then held out his hand to Meli. "Sorry I ran you over, Meli. Forgive me?"

Meli looked like she was about to cry, and not over any injury. She fiddled with her long braid, twisting it around and around. Her eyes were wide and glistening and her lower lip trembled. "Listen, Mr. Romero, the truth is—"

Meli was about to blow our cover!

We were fourth down and needed a big play.

"Bee!" I screamed, then ran away as fast as I could. I waved my arms as if a bee were buzzing around my head. I was allergic to bees, so unfortunately it was a move I was familiar with. Soon Dad was chasing me, followed by Meli, Evy, and the boys, who had hopped out of their cart. Dad always carried an EpiPen in a waist pack and he had it out and ready to go. I'd only ever been jabbed with an EpiPen once, back in third grade after a bee stung my hand during PE. It wasn't fun.

"Ah!" I screamed, running faster.

"Roxy, stop!" Evy yelled.

"Did it get you? Did the bee get you?" Dad was shouting.

I ran on and on, past the potted palms, over the bags of mulch, under the table with the orchids on display, and back into the air-conditioned store. I tucked into a shelf behind the mini-refrigerators and caught my breath.

My brain rattled through a million possibilities.

Maybe Evy would decide that dealing with an anxious, allergic kid like me was just too much. Maybe Dad would realize that things were easier when it was just the three of us.

Or maybe they'd think that I was lost forever at the home improvement store and understand they were better off without me. They'd leave together and build their new house and forget I ever existed. Suddenly it felt hard to breathe, as if I'd really been stung by a bee.

I took big breaths, trying to calm myself. In through my nose and out through my mouth, like Dr. Nordan and I had practiced last week. Slowly, my brain whirred a little less and I started to feel better.

That's when I heard an employee on the overhead speakers announce, "Roxana Romero, please meet your parents at the customer service desk or ask an employee for help."

Carefully, I stepped out from behind the boxes. Meli was standing there.

"Hey," she said. "Are you okay?"

"Yeah, I'm fine. No bee stings. Just part of the plan, right?" My voice cracked. I wanted to hide behind the boxes again.

Meli tugged on my sleeve as if she knew what I was thinking. "Maybe we just need to make some adjustments. No more pretending to be hurt. We want to break our parents up, not give them heart attacks. My mom already worries enough about my scoliosis."

"Deal," I said. "How'd you find me, anyway?"

Meli shrugged. "When everyone started running I just stopped and watched the security screens, searched for a kid in a football jersey, and there you were. You were a blur, you ran so fast!" She pointed to screens near the ceiling. One camera was pointed right at us. I waved. Meli waved too. We both giggled.

"We'd better go," she said. Meli walked ahead. She had tied a bright pink feather into her hair that morning. It looked nice, and I wondered if she had more feathers she might share with me.

Our parents came into view, and both Dad and

Evy rushed at me and patted me all over. "Are you okay? How's your breathing?" Dad asked.

"The bee didn't get me. It just freaked me out," I said.

Dad touched my cheek and gave me a worried look. "Listen, Roxy, if your feelings get to be too much, you have to let me know."

"They weren't," I lied. "I just didn't want to get stung."

Evy reached down and held my hand. That's all. She just held my hand and gave it a little squeeze. When she let go, I nearly reached out to take it again, but I stopped myself. Evy wasn't my mom. She didn't understand anything about me, and it would do the Disaster Plan no good to forget that. The sooner Evy and Dad broke up, the better it would be for all of us.

Back at the new house, we unloaded the supplies. The plumber had done a good job. He'd set up big fans overnight and the house was dry again. Evy and Dad got to work installing a new ceiling fan in the living room. The old one had shorted out when the pipe burst. The boys played in their bedroom while Meli and I went outside to check out the trampoline.

We took off our shoes and climbed up. The trampoline was covered in mahogany leaves and palm fronds. We swept it clean with our hands in silence, then sat down on opposite sides, our feet almost touching.

I wiggled my toes. "I'm glad your toe isn't really broken," I said.

"And I'm happy you weren't stung by a bee."

"Yeah, that would have actually been really bad." We were quiet for a little while, both of us lost in our thoughts. It felt good to sit there with Meli, like we were actual friends. Was this a . . . truce? The Disaster Plan may have triggered a ceasefire between us, but I knew it was temporary. As soon as our mission was accomplished we could both go back to our regular lives.

Overhead, blue jays squawked in the trees, and a screech owl started hooting. "I think we need to establish official rules for this Disaster Plan," I said at last.

Meli nodded. "Number one, like we said earlier—no hurting anybody or pretending to get hurt."

"Agreed. Also, no hurting anyone's feelings on purpose," I added.

"That's two. Number three, don't involve the Bens. This is our plan, and they'll just mess it up," Meli said.

We thought for a bit. I remembered how Meli almost spilled the beans. "Number four, the Disaster Plan is top secret. No caving, no matter what, or we'll never get our old lives back."

Meli got to her feet and started bouncing. "Number five!" she shouted, breathless. "We work together. On everything."

I stood and started bouncing too, and soon we were jumping in the same rhythm, going higher and higher with each jump. It felt like we might touch the sky and fly off, Meli back to her old house, and me back to mine. We could do it if we kept to the rules, I just knew it.

CHAPTER 7
MELI

"Moving is the worst," Mami mumbled for what felt like the twentieth time. I nodded a little too enthusiastically as I took a box of Ben's books into the Romero's driveway. We'd spent the whole week going back and forth between Roxy's place and the fixer-upper, packing up all the stuff that Carlos had insisted wouldn't take long because they were "just a few things."

He couldn't have been more wrong, which was perfect. It made our parents so on edge that the Disaster Plan went on autopilot, taking on a life of its own.

"We need more tape and we're out of Bubble

Wrap!" Mami shouted to Carlos as he headed to the store for the third time today. "And see if you can get a few more boxes!"

Carlos stopped to check his watch and shook his head. "The movers will be here in an hour. We'll never be ready."

"¿Ya ves? You should've let me make a list, amor," Mami said in a singsongy voice. Carlos looked the way I felt every time Mami said *I told you so*, like he was trying real hard to bite his tongue.

The Benjamins had been sent to play at Abuela's house so they wouldn't get in the way once the movers came. Roxy and I were in the living room folding last night's bedsheets, but she kept twisting them before I could grab the corners.

"Quit it," I said, wanting to get our chores over with.

Roxy gave me a smile that looked more like a bite, and through her teeth said, "I'm *helping*, remember?"

"Oh, right." Sometimes I couldn't tell if Roxy was naturally annoying or pretending to be. Was there really a difference?

I grinned as sweetly as I could muster and turned to Carlos. "Our storage container was packed and delivered in no time thanks to Mami's planning and organization," I said. Carlos grabbed his car keys, took a deep breath, and told Mami to text him if she thought of anything else.

"Nice assist, Ms. Know-It-All!" Roxy whispered. As usual, I had no idea what sport she was referencing, but based on how distraught her dad looked I could tell we'd definitely scored another point for our Disaster Plan. But then slowly, as the hours passed and her house got emptier and emptier, Roxy grew quiet. No amount of our parents' bickering seemed to satisfy her.

"You okay?" We'd gone into her room one last time to make sure nothing was forgotten. But already it seemed like everything had been: the blue sky her mom had painted now hovered over a wide, empty space. The crescent moon in the corner looked lonely, as if it had no one left to watch over.

Roxy took off the Marlins baseball cap she'd been wearing all morning and started pulling at the strap.

"Yeah. It's just . . . whoever moves in will probably paint the walls. And it'll be like me and my mom were never here."

I knew what she meant. No matter how many times Mami tried to tell me that our new life together was a blank canvas—something we could make our own—I couldn't help feeling like someone had taken a giant eraser to all our memories. On the day we'd moved out of our house, James, Janette, and I had triple pinky swore that we'd be JMJ forever. It'd been our secret name for years, like BFF, but with our initials. But now that it was summer and we weren't neighbors anymore, I hadn't seen them in over a week. I wondered what kind of fun they'd gotten into without me.

"We'll get it all back soon," I said, hoping to reassure not only her but me. "Didn't you see how much our parents disagreed all day? And that was just you guys moving out! Imagine how bad it'll be once we all move in."

"Yeah. I guess." She shrugged and dimmed the switch as we left, barely looking back. We climbed into Carlos's car and followed the moving truck to the fixer-upper.

Everyone was quiet the whole way until my phone rang. It was Janette! Maybe I'd been missing her so much that she sensed it. Mami always said people's energies have a way of aligning.

I pressed answer and when our faces showed up on the screen, Janette gasped as if it had been ages. "We miss you! We're going to an escape room at the Falls today. Can you come?"

Mami shook her head no in the front seat. The Falls was one of my favorite places in all of Miami. It was an outdoor mall, but it looked like a tropical paradise, with rock grottos, water fountains, and palm trees that were wrapped in white lights, so it felt like the holidays year-round.

"Please, Mami?" I begged, leaning toward the car's center console.

"I'm sorry, Meli, but there's too much to do today."

I plopped back into my seat and sighed. "Maybe you and James can come over instead and we can pretend to escape the new house!" I said, loud enough for everyone in the car to hear.

Roxy giggled but Mami gave me a very serious look, and Carlos glanced at me through the rearview mirror.

"That's not a nice thing to say on our first day at the new house," he said, in a tone I'd only ever heard him use on his *own kids*. The top of my cheeks grew warm, like tears were rushing to the back of my eyes. Who'd given him permission to pretend to be my dad?

"I was just joking," I said. Even though I wasn't, not entirely.

"It was worth a shot," Janette said. "I gotta go. Call me later? I want to see your room!"

I ended the call as we pulled up to the house. Abuela had just arrived too to drop off our brothers, and between them and us and the moving truck beeping real loud as it backed into the driveway, I felt like I might explode if I didn't get to someplace quiet soon.

Benji ran into the living room holding Abuela's

Yorkie, Kiwi, on a leash, while Ben trailed behind them with a pink cardboard box in his hands.

"These two!" Abuela gestured to the Bens as she kissed Mami and Carlos hello on the cheeks. "¡Son unos angelitos!"

Roxy and I rolled our eyes and pretended to barf. Of course our brothers would act like perfect angels.

"We went to the park and then we gave Kiwi a bath and then Abuela took us to get donuts!" my brother said, nearly out of breath.

"We brought your favorites," Ben added quietly. "Jelly filled for Roxy and chocolate glazed for Meli."

"That's so thoughtful of you, mijito," Mami said.

Since when did Mami call Roxy's brother "my son"? I wished she and Carlos would stop acting like they'd swapped places. He wasn't my dad, and she wasn't Ben's mom, period. I grabbed a napkin and a donut and made a beeline for the stairs, but Mami stopped me.

"No food in your bedrooms; you know the rules."

"Speaking of bedrooms," Carlos said. "The boys

have already agreed they'll share a room, which leaves the two bedrooms across the hall for you girls. We leave it up to you to agree on which bedroom is whose." He was doing that firm, deep thing with his voice again. I'd lost my appetite for the donut.

"Sure, Dad. We've got this!" Roxy said in a much more cheerful tone than I was expecting. She grabbed my arm and dashed up the stairs before he could even reply. I ran as hard as I could to keep up with her. We walked through one empty bedroom that was dark and faced the street in front of the house, then through the Jack and Jill bathroom that connected it to the other room. We both gasped as we stepped inside.

This bedroom overlooked the pool and the trampoline, and the sun shone through the windows in a way that made it feel like summer inside. I could already imagine placing my yoga mat in the corner.

"This is perfect," Roxy said.

"Oh no. I see where this is going." Of course Roxy would want the same room as I did, which meant, as usual, she'd probably get her way. "You're going to beg your dad for the good room, aren't you? And it's not like he ever says no to you—"

"Wait, what's that supposed to mean? Are you calling me spoiled?"

"If the flip-flop fits," I said, looking down at her University of Miami sandals.

"Jealous?" She stretched out one foot and pointed her toes. The green-and-orange straps weren't at all my style, but maybe I was jealous, a little. Mami would never let me wear shoes like that. She'd say they don't have enough arch support and would be bad for my back.

"You just have it so easy. You have no idea what it's like to live with the kind of rules I do," I said.

"It's not my fault that my dad's nice to me and your mom's so strict."

"Don't talk about my mom that way."

"Then don't say my dad spoils me!" She'd gotten really loud really fast, and it seemed to surprise both of us. "Sorry." She sighed. "We need to focus. What I was *trying* to say is that this can work for our plan. We can't help it if we both want the same room."

"But we'll get in trouble again if we fight over it."

Roxy rubbed her hands together. "That's the best part. We don't fight over it. We present our case to our parents and let them fight over it. Like on lawyer shows on TV. My dad will take my side, like you said, and your mom . . . will she take yours?"

"Probably. But even if she doesn't, she'll be annoyed your dad spoils you," I teased.

"He doesn't . . . whatever." Roxy rolled her eyes. "Let's just get this over with."

We hurried back downstairs, where we found Mami and Carlos telling the movers where to place all the boxes and furniture. The Benjamins were on their knees in the living room scrubbing a wet spot on the carpet.

"Kiwi is perfectly house-trained," Abuela said. "But even she has accidents, I guess."

"Can't blame her for mistaking this place for a bathroom," Roxy whispered to me.

I tried to hold back a chuckle.

"That was fast," Mami said. "Did you decide which rooms you want?"

We looked at each other, nodded in unison, and blurted out at the same time:

"The one facing the pool!"

"The one facing the street!"

Wait. WHAT? We were supposed to have picked the same room!

"Um, excuse us one second!" I pulled at Roxy's sleeve until we were both in the garage. "I thought you wanted the one in the back!" I hissed. It was obviously the best one.

Roxy scrunched her face and adjusted her teal jersey. "Why would I want all the sun in my eyes? Besides, I like seeing people and cars go by around the neighborhood. I thought *you* wanted the room by the *front* of the house."

I groaned. "No way! It's too dark in there. It would be so bad for my art."

She ran both hands through her hair in frustration. "So what are we supposed to do? Switch so we each get our version of the bad room?"

We were trapped. No way was I going to get stuck in a depressing cave for the sake of our Disaster Plan. And I knew Roxy was too stubborn to let go of the room she wanted. "You tell me. This was *your* genius idea."

"You're the one who went along with it."

"Girls! What's the holdup?" Carlos had come into the garage to toss another empty box onto the recycle pile. Mami followed behind him. "Is it all settled with the rooms or what?"

We stared long and hard at each other. I didn't blink. Finally, Roxy looked away and said, "Yeah. I'll get the one facing the street."

"And I'll get the one in the back," I mumbled.

"Don't sound so sad," Mami said. "Aren't those the rooms you wanted?"

We nodded.

"Great. We'll get them painted next week," Carlos said. "I'm glad you agree even though you disagree."

"Like night and day," Mami added. "Complementary opposites."

I frowned, offended my mom would think Roxy and I went well together. And the way Carlos was talking, you'd think we were about to declare world peace.

Still, even though this attempt had backfired, I couldn't help being a little relieved. The rooms *were* perfect for each of us, in their own unique ways.

The next morning Mami said she had a special surprise. She seemed so excited about showing it to us during breakfast that she reminded me of a kid doing show-and-tell in kindergarten, buzzing with energy.

"As you know, fixing up a house *and* planning a wedding are really big undertakings. So I've been thinking of ways we can make sure things go smoothly from now on." She was hugging several notebooks and folders close to her chest, and I could see little tabs sticking out of the pages. "I present you with: The Official Flores-Romero Fixer-Upper and Wedding Master Plans!" She held them up high and started humming what I can only describe as a kind of theme song for them.

"Plans. Plural, huh?" Carlos's face disappeared as

he took a big sip of his coffee. "That's great, amor. But I thought we already had plans."

Mami's eyes went wide. "Yes, but these are new and improved! It's not just the wedding that's coming up soon. School will start again before you know it! This house needs to be ready for homework and school projects and four times the laundry! And we need to get the backyard picture-perfect for the ceremony and send out wedding invitations!"

"Whoa. Invitations? Already?" Roxy asked. She held a spoonful of Cheerios halfway to her mouth, looking straight at me.

"Like, to actual people?" I didn't like the sound of that at all. "That makes the wedding feel so . . . real."

"Exactly." Mami nodded, flipping to the first page in her planner.

Carlos put his arm around Mami's waist and kissed her cheek. "You're absolutely right. Thank you for keeping us all on task."

I nearly choked on my orange juice. Had Mami and Carlos magically gotten on the same page? That wasn't good. I tried not to imagine their wedding date on our families' calendars in black, permanent ink. It was time we made our parents' to-do list a big old to-don't. "I guess we better get to work," I said, and Mami started her presentation.

I could see Roxy growing tense in her seat the more complicated it got. It was complete with a color-coded calendar, a checklist of tasks for each of us, and a daily schedule planned to the last minute. So much for our Disaster Plan—Mami's organization skills were threatening to destroy it all.

"What do you think? Boys, Meli? ¿Listos?"

Ben flipped carefully through one of Mami's binders. "It's so pretty."

I nodded, pretending to be onboard. "Yup. Ready."

"Okay," Carlos said. "Go brush your teeth and let's get to work."

In our bathroom, as I placed toothpaste on my toothbrush and then Roxy's, I brainstormed ways to make Mami's plans for a "smooth" home renovation as bumpy as a Rocky Road sundae, but everything felt so complicated. "Maybe we just keep things simple. Mami's got all those to-do lists, so we start there but do everything wrong. By accident, of course. Or better yet, like Amelia Bedelia!"

Roxy spat into the sink. "Amelia who?"

"Bedelia. From the books? She takes everything literally, like when they tell her to put the lights out, she places a bunch of lightbulbs outside the house."

"That sounds hilarious. And chaotic," Roxy said.

We tapped our toothbrushes together like they were cups. "Exactly."

It turned out that Carlos wanted me to help him with some yard work and Mami was hoping to get Roxy's opinion on the Pinterest boards she'd created for the kitchen and bathrooms.

"It'd be a shame if you picked out something really gross and tacky," I reminded her.

"Make a mess out there," Roxy said. I nodded and we headed downstairs.

"Your dad told me you like going to open houses with him," I heard Mami say to Roxy, just as Carlos handed me a hat, a bottle of sunscreen, and some gloves. Jealousy squirmed its way back to a little corner of my mind. How come Roxy got to help pick out new tiles and light fixtures while I got stuck with dirty work? Literally. Out front, Carlos pulled out a wheelbarrow full of dark, moist soil. He signaled for me to follow him to his car, and when he opened the trunk, it was full of dozens of pots of plants and flowers.

"The people at the nursery said these plants would look good along the entryway," he said. "I could really use your help with the landscape design, though."

"Me? I don't know that much about plants." But making a mess of the yard would be easy.

"Meli. I've seen your paintings and sculptures. You have an amazing use of color. The way you put certain shades and hues together. It's very original."

Maybe it was just the sun, but my cheeks grew warm, melting away some of the cold feelings I'd been having toward Carlos. I worked really hard on choosing the colors for my pieces. I didn't think anyone noticed.

"Oh. Thanks." I pulled my hat lower to cover my face and took in all the different leaves and flower petals. I'd never thought of art and plants going together, but when he put it like that, I started to think of the plants like a paint palette. The large bed of dirt in front of the house was our blank canvas.

We spent the next couple of hours digging holes and wiggling each plant out of its plastic pot, placing it gently into the dirt. It was so nice to be creating something with my hands again, I forgot all about the Disaster Plan. Carlos and I arranged the flowers in bright clusters of yellows and pinks that lined the entryway, and then against the front walls of the house, we grouped several large, leafy plants in every shade of green imaginable, from lime to dark olive.

"It looks so cheerful and welcoming," I said when we were done. Carlos brought out the hose to water our creation.

"Just wait a few weeks. They'll look even more beautiful once they take root. That's when they really get a chance to flourish," he said.

Through the window beyond the bushes we'd just planted, I could see Roxy and Mami huddled close on the couch, pointing at something on Mami's laptop. Roxy nodded excitedly, and for the first time all week, she looked relaxed. I hadn't noticed until now that Roxy usually had her guard up, as if deep down she was scared that something could go wrong.

A cold splash of water startled me, and I yipped in surprise.

"Gotcha!" Carlos laughed. I ducked out of the path of the hose.

"No fair! I wasn't ready!"

Mami and Roxy ran out of the house to see what the commotion was about, and soon the boys had poured out into the yard too.

"Water fight!" they yelled. Benji filled a plastic cup with water and tossed it in our direction. Ben one-upped him with a bucket that he'd found in the garage.

We were all soaked and out of breath by the time the sun started setting, so we sat on the front porch and watched the sky change colors. Mami leaned into Carlos as he placed his hand on her knee.

"Mi amor, I'm afraid water shenanigans and watching the sunset weren't on today's to-list," he said. A bubbly giggle escaped Roxy's lips, and it traveled over us like the wave at a football game.

"That's true," Mami said. "But we still accomplished a lot."

I was about to agree when I imagined all of the tasks on Mami's list being canceled out by me and Roxy's schemes, and for the first time since our Disaster Plan started, I felt guilty. It stung like a tiny mosquito bite at the end of a muggy day. I slapped the skin on my shoulder and snapped out of it.

Don't be deceived, I thought. *Just because we're happy now doesn't mean we won't be miserable forever.*

CHAPTER 8
ROXY

Was the water fight in the front yard a blast?

Yup.

Did it look a little bit like we were a family?

Yup again.

Would it do?

Not at all.

Over breakfast the next morning Meli and I took our time eating until the two of us were the last ones at the breakfast bar. Evy had left her planner on the counter. It was a bulging notebook, with brochures and sticky notes poking out from between the pages. She'd written *Master Plan* in swirly cursive writing on the cover. I took a sticky note and covered "Master," then scribbled *Disaster* in its place.

"Don't do that," Meli said, peeling the note off and crumpling it up.

"You're no fun."

"Correct. That's me. 'No-Fun Meli.'" She slurped her cereal milk, sending awful tingles down my spine. I *hated* mouth sounds.

"Hmph. Sure seemed like you were 'Super-Fun Meli' in the garden with my dad yesterday."

She dropped her spoon into her bowl with a loud clink. "Jealous?"

"Shut up," I said. Truthfully, I *was* a little bit jealous, even if the water fight had been fun.

A little corner of light blue paper was sticking out of Evy's planner. I pulled it out. At the top of the page it read *Together with their families* in cursive. It took me a second to make out the cursive, which I wasn't used to reading. Beneath that, it read *Eva and Carlos request the pleasure of your company at their marriage.* On the bottom were the words *August first, at our new home."*

"Ugh," I said, showing the invitation to Meli.

"Double ugh," Meli replied. "That's—" She stopped to count on her fingers. "Forty-six days away!"

Just then Dad came back to the kitchen to refill his coffee mug. Quickly, I tucked the invitation back into Evy's planner. Dad blew steam off the top of his mug and peered at us. "What's the plan for today? There's stuff to unpack, dusty corners to sweep out, new siblings to bond with." Dad winked and my heart sank. He was so happy.

Meli slung an arm around my shoulders. "Bonding!"

"That's my girl," Dad said, and tousled Meli's hair before leaving us alone again. I pushed Meli's arm from my shoulder.

"Get off me," I grumbled.

Meli shrugged. "Can't have Carlos suspecting anything." Then she shoved a spoonful of soggy cereal into her mouth.

It was time to kick our Disaster Plan into high gear. It was already June and August first would be here before we knew it!

"Ever had bats in your house?" I asked.

She spit out her cereal. "No way. So gross!"

"It is," I said, grinning. "We had them one time and it was the worst. They were in the walls and attic. You could hear them scrambling from behind the walls and overhead all day long. Dad flipped out completely. There was a baby one in the living room and Ben almost picked it up before Dad stopped him. Can you imagine? I thought Dad was going to faint. You know how Indiana Jones hates snakes? Well, Dad hates bats the same way."

Meli frowned. "I don't know who Indiana Jones is, but I believe you. So what, we go catch bats or something?"

I had to pause. First, Meli had never seen *Indiana Jones*? She didn't even know who he was? Second, did she really think I was proposing we trap real bats?

"No. We *pretend* to be bats."

Meli looked confused. "Costumes? We're too big to be bats, Roxy."

I slapped my forehead in frustration. "No. Listen. We get into the attic and start scratching. Dad is going to think it's bats again and will want to evacuate the premises immediately just from the sound alone!"

Meli brightened. "That sounds great. But what happens when he realizes the house is bat-free?"

"Don't you see? The chaos before the realization is what's important. What matters is that we are relentless! Exhausting! Wear them down, Meli. A good offense is the best defense!"

Meli swirled her cereal around with her spoon. "Your dad is really nice, you know?"

That took me aback. It almost sounded like Meli was starting to like my family. I stopped myself from saying anything about Evy, who was actually really sweet despite how strict she could be sometimes. "Evy is great too but we can't let anything hold us back," I said at last. "They'll thank us later. You'll see."

The next thing I knew, Meli and I had climbed into the attic using a ladder that dropped down from the ceiling. It wasn't really an attic, though, not like the ones I'd seen in movies. It was more of a crawl space. That's how houses are built in Florida thanks to all the hurricanes we get. It doesn't make sense to put a big old empty hat on a house that the wind can take off. It was suffocating and dark in the crawl space. Thankfully Meli brought a flashlight with her, which she pulled out of a small backpack she was wearing. We crawled past boxes the old owners had left behind until we were directly above my dad and Evy, talking in the upstairs bathroom where Evy was hanging up a new shower curtain. We listened as their conversation floated up to where we sat.

"Ya ves, Carlos, the girls are getting along great," Evy was saying.

We couldn't hear my dad's response. The thing was, Meli and I *were* getting along well. Just last night she'd offered to put my hair into French braids so that it would be wavy in the morning, and I'd let her. Not once did she tug too hard or criticize my flyaways. She just worked in silence, humming a little song. It was . . . nice. Like we'd always done things like that.

I shook my head, trying to focus. We were only getting along because the Disaster Plan temporarily put us on the same team. Moments like last night weren't real, and things would go back to normal before long.

I pulled the two forks I'd brought with me out of my jean pockets. "Here," I said to Meli. "Use these."

Slowly I raked the forks against the wooden floor of the crawl space, tapping every so often. It sounded just like the bats in our old house. "You start over there," I whispered to Meli. She crawled a few feet away and got to work. Sweat was falling into my eyes as we scraped and scraped, hoping Dad would notice. Then, at last:

"Evy. Evy, shh. What's that noise?"

Meli was grinning like a supervillain. She scratched harder.

"I don't hear anything," we heard Evy say.

"Oh, no. No, no, no," Dad started to say, getting louder by the minute. "I know what that is!"

"Carlos, the shower curtain!"

"We can put it up later," we heard Dad argue.

Evy groaned. "If we leave it for later it will never get done!"

As they went back and forth, Meli and I quickly pocketed the forks. Then Meli did the most surprising thing. She zipped open her backpack and pulled out three brunette Barbies. She yanked the heads off the dolls. She held them in the palms of her hand, their brown hair all swirled together. "Bats. See? At least in the dark and from a distance they might look like bats."

I gave Meli the biggest hug. "You're a weird genius, do you know that?" Meli laughed, then strategically placed the Barbie heads on the floor. They really did look like small brown creatures in the gloomy attic!

Quick as a flash, we climbed down the ladder and popped it back in place. Just under the clock, too, because Dad and Evy turned the corner then.

"Did you hear any scratching?" Dad asked, breathless. He was pale and was hugging himself.

"Yup," I said. "Meli did too. Sounded just like that time we had—"

"Don't say it!" Dad shouted. He shivered all over, took a deep breath, then started to pull down the ladder.

"Vámonos," Meli whispered, and the two of us left the hall.

Moments later, Dad must have spotted the doll heads because he yelped. "Bats! Why'd it have to be bats?"

Meli and I were in the living room, debating in whispers when to go retrieve the Barbie heads, when Dad and Evy had their first big, explosive fight.

"Poison, Evy. Poison will finish them off in no time," Dad shouted.

"Pues no, Carlos. I'm drawing a line. An expert can come and remove the little creatures without killing them!" Evy shouted back.

"¿Que expert, ni expert?" Dad said. "What if they leave one behind? Don't be ridiculous."

"RIDICULOUS?" Evy said, her eyes bugging out. "Bats don't hurt people. I didn't realize I was engaged to a scaredy-cat!"

Dad gasped. "They absolutely *can* hurt people! A sick bat can bite you and you wouldn't even know it. And then, fuácata—you're a goner!"

"I didn't know I was engaged to a *bat expert*," Evy said loudly.

Meli reached over and grabbed my hand. "I don't like this," she whispered.

Grateful, I squeezed her hand back. I didn't like it either. In fact, my heart was starting to beat too fast, and my eyes were stinging.

Dad got quiet then. He stopped and took a big breath. "I'm sorry for yelling, Evy. Bats just freak me out."

Evy stepped closer to Dad and put her arms around him. "You aren't a scaredy-cat, mi amor. You're the bravest man I know."

Beside me, Meli sighed deeply. I let out a big breath too. Watching them fight had felt . . . weird. But isn't a fight what we had wanted?

"Let's not do anything else today, okay?" Meli said.

I nodded in agreement.

In the end, Evy won the bat battle. Dad found a guy online called Bill the Bat Wrangler, who showed up wearing safari gear and carrying a beach chair. We watched as Bill climbed into the attic (we'd taken the Barbie heads down earlier) and descended with an actual dead baby bat in his gloved hands.

The boys were with us, and Bill showed them the bat. "Cool! Can we touch it?" they both said at once.

"No way, guys," Dad said.

"This here is guano, a.k.a. bat poop," Bill said, showing off the tiny brown poops in his other hand.

Benji reached out to touch it and Evy grabbed him by the wrist. "No touching. But did you know, kids, that guano was Peru's main export one hundred years ago? And the ancient Incas used it to fertilize crops! ¿Interesante, no?"

Dad did another full-body shiver. "Gross, no?" he said. Evy gave Dad a serious look. "And yes, muy interesante también," he added.

Bill nodded enthusiastically. "There was definitely a nest up there at some point. But since y'all heard scratching, I'm going to assume a new bat family has moved in. If you don't mind, I'm going to camp out in your backyard to watch when they leave at night and determine how they're getting out. Then I'll patch up the places where they exit so that they can't come back in."

"And no bats get hurt?" Evy asked, anxious.

"No ma'am," Bill the Bat Wrangler said.

Dad let out a big breath. "I'd shake your hand, but you're holding . . . stuff," he said, pointing to the dead bat and the poop.

Bill smiled. "I understand. It's why I wear gloves." He shook the guano off his gloved hand and onto the grass. "The Incas weren't wrong. It's great fertilizer. Thank me later!" Then he set up his gear in the backyard.

I felt Meli tugging me away from everyone. When we were out of earshot, she spun to face me. "There were bats up there at one point, Roxy. Actual bats. OMG."

A shiver ripped through me. "Even if Bill doesn't see any new bats leave, he'll probably patch up any holes so new ones can't get in. I guess our prank did everyone a favor then." I remembered how easy we'd made it for our parents when we each chose a different bedroom. "We've got to stop doing that."

Meli nodded. "For sure. Tomorrow, how about we—"

"Melisa!" Evy interrupted. We looked over to where she was standing, holding a cell phone in the air. "Es tú papá."

"Papi?" Meli squealed, and ran toward her mother, snatching the phone. I watched as Meli wandered around the yard talking with her father, moving her free hand around as she chatted. It reminded me of how I hadn't spoken to my mom in weeks. She was never able to come to the phone. It was always Abuelo who had to pass along messages from her. And when I did talk to her, I was sure I didn't look as happy as Meli did as she listened to her papi. She was lucky, I guess.

I waited until the conversation ended. Meli returned the phone to her mother. I expected her to come back to where I sat so we could brainstorm our next prank. But instead she went inside, walking slowly, her head down. I'd recognize the feelings that went with that walk anywhere.

Whatever her papi had told her, I'm guessing it wasn't good news.

"Hey, wait," I called, and followed her into the house.

"Leave me alone, Roxy," Meli said, sensing me behind her.

"We were going to plot another disaster, remember?" I was trying to distract her, get her mind off the conversation with her papi.

Meli climbed the stairs two steps at a time.

"Hold up!"

Suddenly, Meli spun to face me. Her cheeks were red and wet. "Papi just ditched me and Benji. No more Legoland. 'Help your mother,' he said. Help her ruin my life? No way."

I didn't know what to say. I knew what it felt like when one of your parents disappointed you in a big way. Mami's depression was clinical, which meant that it came and went. And even though it wasn't her fault, sometimes I blamed her for not being there for me and Ben. I'd get angry at her, then sad. Missing her hurt worse than a cramp, worse than getting blitzed as a quarterback. Worse than anything.

I should have kept my mouth shut, but in true Roxy fashion, I made things more terrible.

"It's just Legoland," I said.

Meli gasped. "You're so . . . so . . . INSENSITIVE!" Then she ran up the stairs. If her bedroom had a door, she would have slammed it shut, but Dad had taken it down that morning to replace the rusty hinges.

I pounded up the stairs after her. "I was only trying to help," I said in the empty doorway. Meli was pacing the room like a trapped tiger.

"You were only trying to butt in. Like always."

"Fine. Be sad on your own."

"Fine!" Meli said.

"Fine!" I repeated, though I didn't know why. I was never good at arguing.

"I swear, Roxana Romero, if you say *fine* one more time, I'll, I'll—"

I didn't stay to hear what Meli would do. I left her upstairs and ran to the backyard, ignoring my dad and Evy asking what happened, and headed for the trampoline.

The Bens were using it, but I evicted them with a single, forceful "OUT." They must have seen something on my face that told them not to argue with me.

It was probably the tears in my eyes.

Just then, I hated Melisa Flores with every ounce of my being. She misunderstood everything I said and did. She thought she was better than me in every way—she was smarter, more SENSITIVE—and she'd completely turned my life upside down.

I was only trying to *help*.

If I were her papi, I wouldn't take her to Legoland either.

I lay down on the trampoline, face to the sky, and just stared up at all that blue, imagining I was somewhere lost in it, high up in the atmosphere. I could fly anywhere. Even to New Jersey, maybe, where Mom and Abuelo were.

Anywhere but here.

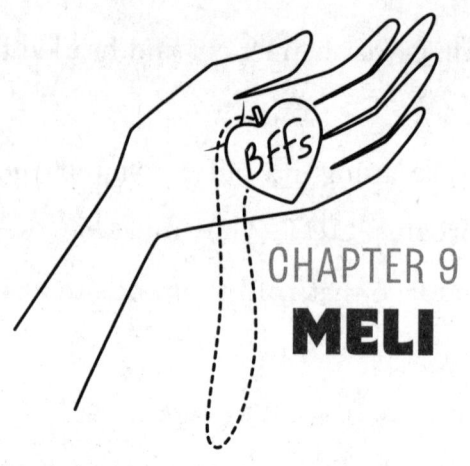

CHAPTER 9
MELI

After my shouting match with Roxy, I thought for sure we'd be grounded, or at least silently guilt-tripped for the next week. Instead, thanks to Carlos convincing Mami that we girls were "going through a lot" and "simply needed a break," I got an even worse punishment: a day for just me and Mami at the South Florida Under the Sun Fun Fair, better known as SFUSFF.

"It'll be like Legoland. Maybe even better, I promise," Mami said right before we pulled into the massive, congested parking lot. "Plus, there might be a couple of surprises . . ."

"Is one of them heatstroke?" I mumbled under

my breath, but Mami was too distracted trying to find a parking spot to notice. It was just as well. She seemed really excited to be here even though I could already think of tons of reasons why this was not going to be, as all the highway billboards promised, *A vacation adventure right at home.*

For one, there was that tongue twister of a name. "South Florida Under the Sun Fun Fair" had more loop-de-loops than any of the fair's rides, and it didn't exactly inspire thoughts of skin care safety. And its acronym—SFUSFF! Whenever I heard the morning news hosts talk about it, I imagined the camera operators wiping spit off the screens.

"They need some SPF to go with that SFUSFF," Roxy had said once over breakfast. I'd laughed so hard I almost choked on my toast. Thinking about it now as Mami and I walked up to the ticket booth, I felt a tightness rising up my neck.

"You okay, Meli?" Mami asked.

I nodded and took a lip balm out of my belt bag to keep from making eye contact. Why did everything have to be a joke to Roxy? Maybe when you got everything you asked for it was easy to make light of other people's problems. I'd had enough of Roxy acting like the things that mattered to me were no big deal. First it'd been my purple pen, then the talent show, and now Legoland. She couldn't put herself in my shoes long enough to see that Papi taking me and Benji to Legoland wasn't *just* about a theme park. It was supposed to hold the few remaining pieces of my life together. Now they were all crumbling over like a tower of falling bricks.

"Can we just go—"

Everything got dark as a pair of hands scooped over my eyes.

"Guess who?!"

I'd know that deep, cracking voice anywhere.

"J!" said another. "You can't just sneak up on people like that!"

"James? Janette?!"

"Surprise!" Mami said.

We hugged and air-kissed on the cheek and did our signature handshakes that consisted of us making two *J*s with our thumb and index fingers, then turning them downward into an *M*.

"JMJ again at last," I said as Mami went to get us tickets. "It feels like it's been forever. I mean, you cut your hair!"

James had grown it out all year so it covered the tips of his ears, but now it was short on the side and his brown curls swooped over his forehead. "It still feels weird. Janette came with me to the barber shop for moral support."

"I think it looks great," I said, trying to ignore the sting of not having been there. A delicate chain on the top part of Janette's ear caught my eye. "Wait a second, when did you get a new piercing?"

"When did you get taller than me?" she teased, standing with her back against mine. James slapped his fingers together and made a hissing sound through his teeth. Then he leaned in so the three of us could take a selfie together. I smiled so big my eyes came out closed, but I didn't care. I felt like finally, I had a part of my old life back.

"Que te parece, Meli? Not as good as Legoland, but not as bad as *SPFFF* or whatever it's called would make you think, right?" Mami said.

We were sitting on a picnic bench by the food trucks while James and Janette waited in line for flan bites. Mami had ordered us corn dogs and funnel cakes with extra powdered sugar on top. The sky was showing off with a purple-orange sunset, and my mom was letting me eat fried food after a day spent riding the MegaDrop four times in a row with my best friends.

"It's perfect, Mami. Thank you. Best day ever," I said, placing my head on her shoulder.

She tapped my knee softly. "I'm glad. Only problem is, now I have to admit to Carlos that he was right. Maybe you and Roxy just needed some time apart to recharge and hit the reset button."

"Reset?" I wished Mami hadn't brought up the Romeros. I was about to say that we weren't robots when her phone rang.

"Dáme un minuto. ¿Alo?" she said, holding up one finger. It was obvious by the way Mami's voice went up in pitch that it was Carlos. "Amor, were your ears burning? Meli and I were just talking about you, wondering how your day with Roxy's going."

That was a stretch. I wasn't the one who had brought up Roxy, and the thought of what she was up to hadn't crossed my mind in at least an hour and a half. Knowing her, she was probably at a football game with her teammates, speaking purely in sports puns by now.

I sighed in relief as Mami walked out of earshot and James and Janette came back with not only flan bites but frozen lemonades. They held a bunch of straws, napkins, cups, and food containers close to their chests to keep from dropping everything.

"So. Now that it's just us, you have to catch us up on all the chisme," Janette said, raising her eyebrows at the mention of juicy gossip. "I want to know all about the new house, and Roxy, and your mom's fiancé."

"You mean the *old* new house," James added. "Roxy's dad must not be a very good real estate agent."

"He's okay. He's not *that* bad," I said.

Janette swirled her lemonade around with a straw and slurped real loud. "What's it like living with Roxy? What does she say when she talks in her sleep?"

My face grew warm. The first night I slept at Roxy's, I'd texted Janette that I'd *bet* Roxy talked in her sleep, and made some other mean assumptions too. I guess Janette had decided they were all true.

"She doesn't, actually," I said.

"I still can't believe she got you kicked out of school early. Ms. Ledero's art club party was legendary. She made Nutella crepes for us," James said.

Nutella crepes? Those were my favorite! "You never told me that!"

"We didn't want you to feel bad about it," Janette said, giving James a sharp stare.

"Sorry. We just miss you, that's all. If it weren't for Roxy we'd still be JMJ, you know?"

I nodded. I must've texted those exact words to our group chat a half dozen times. All these weeks, the only thing I'd wanted was some time with my best friends. Time to be me and not pretend I was fine just to make Mami and Benji feel better about our ugly new house. Time to vent to J and J about how Roxy and her cheesy dad and her goody-goody brother were not like me and my family *at all.*

"It's kind of a catastrophe. Every day, just one after the other." I told them all about the bat poop in the attic, and how Papi had canceled on us from an ocean away, and the fight Roxy and I had after. "*Be sad on your own.* She actually said that to me." It hurt to repeat Roxy's words out loud. "As if I haven't already been doing that all summer, feeling completely alone while she and her dad bulldoze through my life and Mami and Benji call it 'building a home.'"

"Oh, Meli. That sounds awful," Janette said.

"The worst," James agreed. "But you're not alone. We're still here for you. Even though we're not, like, next door."

"It's not the same, though, is it?" I couldn't believe I was about to burst into tears right next to the funnel cake stand.

"There has to be something we can do to get you

out of this!" Janette was starting to sound angrier than the time her big sister de-alphabetized her bookshelves just to get back at her for borrowing a shirt without asking. I wanted to say something to calm her down, but it was the one thing I wasn't supposed to say.

After all, we'd promised. The Disaster Plan was top secret.

But what did it matter to Roxy who I told, or what I did when I was *on my own*? Unlike her, my friends cared about my feelings. They wanted to help instead of just making fun of my problems.

"The thing is . . ." I signaled for them to huddle close. "We've been working on a plan to get our old lives back." Then I told them everything. The whole plan, the many ways it'd failed, and how Mami now had a master plan that, for all we knew, was the kryptonite to our Disaster Plan.

"So basically I'm starting to think I'm doomed," I finished, feeling about as sad as the giant stuffed bunnies that stared at us from the prize booths. J and J sat next to me on top of the picnic table and sandwiched me in a hug. For a few moments we said nothing at all, and it was nice, for once, to let the quiet speak for us. There was no need to try to change the subject to cheer me up. James and Janette just let me feel bad for a little while, and somehow that made me feel better.

"Que lindos," Mami said, taking a picture of us now that she'd finally hung up the phone. James and Janette let me go.

"What'd Carlos say?" I asked, tossing my empty paper plate and cup in the trash.

"Oh, you know, just that they're having a good time. Roxy te manda saludos," Mami added.

James and Janette gave me knowing looks. *Te manda saludos* was one of those things adults always said to be polite, but we knew what it really meant. Translation: *Roxy didn't really say hi or ask about you at all.*

Which was totally and completely fine by me.

Mami did a little shoulder shimmy as she started going through her purse. It was her version of a happy dance, the one she did when she got really good news or checked a big item off her to-do list. I was almost afraid to ask.

"What else did Carlos say?"

Her face lit up. "That our wedding invitations are en route to our friends and family! Look how cute." She showed me a picture of a stack of envelopes with the *love* stamp on them, in what was probably Carlos's hand, judging by the hairy fingers. "I asked him to drop them off at the post office this morning, since it was on his way." Her words came out fast and chipmunk-like from how giddy she was.

"Wow! That's a really big deal," Janette finally said. I was close to tasting a second helping of my flan bites in my throat.

"¡Gracias, Janettita! The wedding's officially official! Now, what next? There's still two hours till the park closes. Why don't you kids catch a few more rides while I watch from here?"

I nodded without saying a word. My breath grew short. My friends looped their arms around mine and stepped into improv mode, pretending everything was good.

"We could go on Pharaoh's Fury. Or the Ring of Fire," James said, wide-eyed as he inhaled the last of his corn dog.

"Or the Bullet Train!" Janette pointed in the direction of the brightest lights.

"Okay, I'll be on this bench," Mami said.

Plotting the rest of my demise, I thought.

James and Janette dragged me down the mulch-lined path toward the giant swing sets and the tents where people were trying to pop balloons with darts.

"Who's next? Pop the balloons to find a hidden prize!" a teen working the dart booth yelled.

I stopped in my tracks. Throwing pointy things at shiny objects sounded like the perfect antidote to all the wedding talk. "I'll go!"

The teen handed me five darts. I took a deep breath and aimed at a purple balloon first. *Pop!* But there was nothing inside. *Pop, pop!* went the white ones next. *Still nothing.* I missed the fourth balloon and focused on a teal one for my last chance: Roxy's favorite color. *Pop!* A gold necklace fell to the floor as the balloon burst.

"Jackpot!" Janette said. "Go, Meli!"

"You got our best prize," the booth attendant said. The necklace had a heart-shaped pendant with the letters *BFFs* engraved on it. When she pinched it with two fingers, it made a little clicking sound. "See? It opens."

"It's a locket! So pretty," Janette said.

I tucked it into my pocket without another glance. Somehow winning a prize with the word *forever* on it was only making me feel worse. "The universe is telling me my life is over. Signed and sealed with a *love* stamp."

We said nothing as we got in line for the Bullet Train. Janette looked over her shoulder at Mami, who wasn't really watching us so much as scribbling in one of her notebooks.

"This is pretty bad," she said. "But you know, people call off weddings all the time! My aunt called off hers on the same day. Her parents were really mad because the guests had already arrived, but then they took the little bride and groom figurines off the top of the cake and replaced them with candles, and we celebrated my uncle's birthday instead. Talk about a surprise party, right?

"My mom hates surprises," I groaned.

"It's not over yet," James said. "If you ask me, you need to put the Disaster Plan into hyperdrive. You and Roxy need to really commit. It's like any risk you take in art or life. You can't do it halfway."

"We weren't doing it halfway," I started to say, but maybe he was right. "I don't know. Maybe deep down we were scared we'd take it too far and get in trouble."

We approached the front of the line and showed our wristbands to the ride operator. The rails of the Bullet Train were Barbie pink, and the carts hissed like a bus stopping in front of a railroad track as people got off, giggling and dizzy.

"I think James has a point," Janette said. "I think whatever you do next has to be like . . . like this roller coaster! Really intense and super unhinged, but when it's over you'll be glad you pulled through. Because otherwise, once they say 'I do,' you'll *really* be stuck on a ride you can't get off from."

We climbed into the cart. The safety bar clicked into place. As the cart started picking up speed, it dawned on me that my friends were right. If we couldn't pull off the Disaster Plan then Roxy Romero would become my sister, and nothing could be worse than that.

I screamed the whole ride through, scared for my life and all the things I wanted back.

CHAPTER 10
ROXY

"Your uncle Al and I used to fight like you and Meli, you know," Dad was saying as he merged onto the highway. "One time he broke my Millennium Falcon toy—"

"Because Uncle Al is a klutz," I interrupted.

"Because Uncle Al is the world's biggest klutz," Dad agreed. "Anyway. I popped the head off his favorite Transformer in revenge, and then we didn't talk to each other for a month." Dad chuckled lightly. "It's how siblings are sometimes."

I didn't say anything because the fact was, Meli was *not* my sibling. Uncle Al and Dad were not only brothers but they were also best friends. Even though he lived in Orlando and we lived in Miami, they had a bond and talked on the phone all the time. They understood each other. Meli was a complete mystery to me nearly always. Whatever her personal playbook was, it was top secret. No matter what I said, I could never predict how she'd react.

The fight we'd had the day before had lodged itself in my throat. It hurt even though Dad had invited Camila and Lucia to join us on a break from "house stuff." As if a trip to the Everglades was going to fix anything.

To make matters worse, the moment I sat down in the car, Dad handed me a stack of envelopes with the word *love* written on them.

"Hold these, Rox? They're the wedding invitations. I need to chuck them into a mailbox."

I was tempted to "chuck" the whole stack out the window.

Dad sidled up to a blue mailbox outside the post office and I handed over the envelopes. "Here," he said, separating two envelopes from the stack and handing them to me. "For Camila and Lucia. They're invited, of course."

"Thanks." If worse came to worst, at least my best friends would be there to witness my life being ruined.

I watched as Dad jiggled the handle on the mailbox to get it open. Just before dropping the envelopes in, he snapped a picture of them on his cell phone.

So cheesy, I thought.

"There," Dad said, texting the photo to Evy. "Now she can check it off that list of hers."

"Evy likes lists."

Dad laughed. "She sure does!"

Doomed, I thought. As soon as everyone received those invitations the wedding would be a done deal.

We pulled into Everglades Vacation Park, just behind a school bus loaded with summer campers. The loose gravel of the parking lot crunched under my sneakers. It was blazing hot, and my shoulders were sizzling under the sun. I glanced over at my dad and his nose and cheeks were white, covered in thick sunscreen. As we walked to the park entrance, I grabbed the sunscreen bottle and slathered some on my arms, face, and legs. Soon I was sticky and smelling like coconuts all over.

Lucia and Camila had already arrived, and they waved at me from where they were standing with their dads. My dad shook hands with theirs, then they went to buy tickets.

"Look at you!" Lucia said, swiping a glob of sunscreen off my nose.

"No smile for your besties?" Camila asked.

I hugged them both as hard as I could. It felt like a million years since I'd hung out with my friends.

"Finally," I said. "A day without Meli, la Melodramática."

Lucia and Camila cracked up at that.

"Every party has a pooper," Camila began.

"And that pooper is Melisa," Lucia finished.

I laughed too, but the goblin in my head had something to say: *Why aren't you defending Meli? She isn't that bad. You're the insensitive one.*

Shh, I told the goblin.

The dads handed us our tickets, including passes to an airboat ride, an alligator wrestling show, and a petting zoo.

"Have fun, girls. Don't become gator lunch," Dad said. "Here's spending money for snacks and a souvenir." He gave me a twenty-dollar bill, then headed off with the other dads to a shady spot in the outdoor café.

I folded the money and put it in my purse. "Evy wouldn't let me and Meli out of her sight for a million bucks," I told my friends.

Camila shrugged. "Forget about it. Your wicked stepmother isn't here now, Cinderella. Let's have fun!"

"She's not wicked. Evy is just . . . strict," I said. "Speaking of Evy . . ." I pulled the invitations from my purse and gave one to each of my friends. "You're invited to the wedding, I guess."

"Don't sound so excited," Camila said.

"It's just that this makes everything—"

"Final," Lucia said. "I get it."

"Yeah."

Lucia made a face, then changed the subject. "Airboat ride first?"

We made our way to the dock. Three airboats bumped lazily against one another. They were flat-bottomed boats, with a massive propeller enclosed in a cage attached to the back. The airboat captain handed us big, plastic earmuffs, then we climbed up onto the benches for passengers. The captain sat on a platform behind us.

"I'm Captain Bucky," he announced into a microphone attached to his T-shirt. "It's about to get loud!" he shouted. "Keep your hands and feet in the boat. I'll point out the gators and other critters. Y'all just keep your eyes peeled. And if you're good, we'll do some 360s out there!" Lucia, Camila, and I held hands as the boat roared to life, then it lurched forward, the prow lifting into the air like an airplane at takeoff.

The three of us screamed but I couldn't hear over the sound of that huge fan. The water all around us looked like a mirror reflecting the blue sky. We rushed past strands of grass on either side of the boat. I thought about Meli and wondered whether she'd like an airboat ride. My throat pinched when I realized I didn't know the answer to that question.

Maybe Meli was right. Maybe I really was insensitive.

The airboat slowed down at last, and Captain Bucky pointed to an alligator in the grass, its mouth wide open. "That's what they do to cool down on hot days. Gators can't pant like a dog or sweat like we do."

Lucia's hand shot up in the air to ask a question. "Are they aggressive?"

The captain shook his head. "Don't bother a gator, and he won't bother you. Can't say the same about a crocodile, though," he said, then held up his hand to show a missing ring finger.

Camila made a gagging sound, and Lucia gasped, "¡Ay!"

Next to us, a mom put her hands over her little boy's eyes.

"Snap! Snap!" Captain Bucky joked. Everyone around me groaned at the joke, and suddenly I was remembering how Meli snapped at me during our fight. I wiggled my fingers, then sat on my hands.

The tour continued and we spotted more gators sunning themselves, a few herons, and an ibis. A cottonmouth swam alongside our boat, fish sparkled just under the surface, and iguanas scurried between the grasses. Captain Bucky kept his promise and we did two 360s. Lucia, Camila, and I clutched each other as the boat spun, feeling like we were about to be flung into the water with the alligators. The airboat rumbled back to the dock, and we got up shakily and gave our earmuffs back to Captain Bucky.

I took one look at my friends and howled with laughter. Their hair was standing up all over, like they'd been electrocuted, and their cheeks were red from the wind.

"You're one to talk," Lucia said. I had put my hair in two braids. I felt them and realized I'd lost a hair tie on the boat ride.

"Bathroom," we all said at once.

Inside, the bathroom was muggy and smelly. There were photographs of alligators on the walls, and all the sinks were dripping. Tiny lizards scampered under the stalls. The mirrors were foggy and scratched, but they would do. Lucia, Camila, and I took turns using Camila's hairbrush.

"Listen, Rox, we've been talking," Lucia said as she tied her hair back into a ponytail. "You've got to do something about this whole stepfamily situation."

"We've barely seen you all summer," Camila added.

"And we're in middle school now. There'll be parties and hangouts at the movies," Lucia continued. "You can't have a stepmom telling you what to do. Not when your dad has been so cool all this time."

"It's not exactly like tha—" I started to say. It was true that Camila and Lucia had invited me twice to the movies, and both times I'd said I couldn't go because Evy was making us help around the house. The truth was, I didn't actually ask her or Dad. I was having too much fun working on the Disaster Plan with Meli.

Camila crossed her arms and pursed her lips and was nodding at everything Lucia said.

"And your dad has to understand that Meli can't replace your friends," Lucia continued.

"He hasn't said that she's replac—"

"Plus, also, asking you to help fix the broken house *they* bought seems inappropriate," Camila emphasized.

"Stop!" I said. Camila's hairbrush clattered to the floor. "I know you're trying to help, but Meli and I have a plan. We have a Disaster Plan, in fact. The wedding isn't going to happen, I promise."

I watched as each of my friends lifted a single, doubtful eyebrow. Lucia waved the invitation in front of her face, using it like a fan. "Oh yeah?" she asked.

"I promise," I insisted. After today, Meli and I were getting serious about the Disaster Plan. No more games. Our old lives were at stake. My friends were right—there was no point in getting distracted by the rare, peaceful, even fun moments between Meli and me.

"Well, tag us in if you need help," Lucia said.

"All for one," Camila added.

"One for all," Lucia and I responded.

We stopped in the gift shop to cool off. Lucia and Camila explored the stuffed animal section while I looked at a shelf with alligator finger puppets. I picked a green one for Ben and a beige one for Benji. The next shelf held mood rings. There was a chart describing what the colors meant. If the stone turned blue, it meant you were happy. Green was calm, black was fearful.

I wish moods were that easy to read, I thought. I put one on my finger. It turned black right away. The alligator finger puppets were four dollars each. The mood rings were five. *Just enough with tax*, I thought, then picked out a ring for Meli too. After we managed to break our parents up, she'd have something to remember me by. And maybe, just maybe, she'd be able to look at my ring and be able to tell what I was really feeling.

A loudspeaker inside the store squealed just as I was paying at the cash register, then the voice of the airboat captain cut in: "Alligator wrestling show in ten minutes! And our alligator nuggets are half off in the café."

"Let's go," I said.

Curious, Camila asked, "What'd you buy?"

"Souvenir for my brother." It was only half a lie. I folded up the bag with the finger puppets and mood rings and shoved it into my purse.

Lucia and Camila followed me outside and we headed to the wrestling show. On the way, I heard Lucia whisper, "I hope Captain Bucky doesn't lose another finger."

CHAPTER 11
MELI

"Shhhh. Be very quiet. Roxy and the boys are sleeping," Mami whispered as we walked into the house. It was way past everyone's bedtime. Even though we'd left the fair before closing, it'd taken another hour or so just to get out of the parking lot. Mami shone her phone's flashlight on the stairs as I tiptoed up the steps; then she opened the linen closet in the hallway and handed me a set of fresh towels.

"Do you need my help with your brace?"

I shook my head. She was probably just as tired as I was, anxious to wash all the day's dirt and grime off her skin, and I didn't want her waiting up for me.

"I think I can manage. I have to learn to put it on by myself eventually, right?"

"Bueno. You just let me know." She kissed me on the forehead and I leaned in to hug her.

"I had fun today. Gracias, Mami."

"Me too. Now sleep tight. You'll need lots of energy for tomorrow." On the way home, she'd explained that tomorrow Roxy and I would be painting our rooms. It'd given me a really good idea for how we could give our Disaster Plan the intensity it'd been missing, and now I couldn't wait to fill Roxy in on all the details. But when I glanced from the bathroom into her room, she was already fast asleep under a mound of blankets and pillows. It was weird seeing her without her usual guard up. Roxy might've been smaller than me, but I always got the sense she was stronger, too, as tireless and forceful on the flag football field as she was off.

Only now she looked calm and vulnerable. It made me wonder what kind of day she'd had. Where had she gone? What had she eaten? Had anyone fun tagged along? I took a shower as quickly and quietly as I could, secretly hoping that the old, creaky pipes in the house would be loud enough to wake Roxy up so we could talk. After putting on a pair of drawstring pants and a white tank top, I stood in front of the mirror and wrapped my brace around my torso. The Velcro straps in the back dangled just out of my reach, but with a few twists and turns I managed to pull them closed. When I climbed into bed, though, it was obvious I hadn't tightened them as well as Mami usually did. I felt like a foot in a big shoe, all that wiggly space making it uncomfortable to move.

"Blerg!" I hissed, undoing the straps and trying to adjust them one more time.

The light from the bathroom flickered on. Roxy was standing at the doorway, rubbing her eyes. Her wavy, tousled hair looked like it'd gotten up before she did. "Do you want me to help?"

I took a moment to think about it. It'd be better than waking up Mami, and it wasn't like Roxy was being mean about it. I was actually relieved and kind of surprised she cared. "I guess. Thanks. Sorry to wake you."

She sat on the edge of my bed and gently pulled on the straps. "It's okay. I wasn't really asleep."

Had Roxy stayed up waiting for me? I turned to face her. Even in the dimmed light I could tell her forehead was a little pink from the sun. "Beach day?" I asked.

"Everglades."

I gasped. "Did you do an airboat ride?"

Roxy nodded.

"I've always wanted to go on one."

"Really?" She made a face like she was seeing two things that didn't go together. Peanut butter and tortilla chips. Ice cream and hot sauce. Meli and airboats.

"Is it really that hard to believe?"

"I just never thought of you as a 'roughing it' type. You're more artsy-smartsy and deep."

"I don't get you sometimes," I said, unsure if she meant that as a compliment or a dig. "If I'm so deep, then how come you assume I'm too shallow to have more than a few interests?"

Roxy shrugged without looking at me. There was a button on my pillowcase that she wouldn't stop picking at. "I don't know. You never seem into any of the things I'm into. I always figured you thought they were silly. Like, maybe you looked down on them. And me."

"*Me* look down on *you*? You're the most popular kid in school, Roxy. Why would you think anyone's looking down on you?"

"You know, being popular doesn't mean everyone likes you," she said defensively. "Or even knows you."

I'd never thought of it that way. My group of friends might have been small, but I'd never doubted that they knew the real me. I thought of the few times I'd interacted with Roxy before our parents got together. She always seemed in a hurry, her mind racing a mile a minute, like she'd rather be hanging out with someone else. "Maybe if you took more time to get to know people," I offered.

"What? That's all I ever do, Meli. Try to make everyone happy. Name one time I was mean to you on purpose." When I didn't say anything, she held up a finger. "One!"

This felt like a trick question, but she glared at me so hard I just blurted out, "My purple pen!"

"What?"

"Last year. You borrowed my purple pen to sign everyone's yearbook and then you never gave it back, not even after our parents started dating, and I kept waiting for you to say something or apologize for stealing it, but it was like it didn't matter to you, like you'd forgotten, even though it was my favorite." The words came out superfast and uncontrollably, like air shooting out of a balloon. My nostrils flared as I caught my breath.

"Your purple pen? Of course I remember." Roxy pursed her lips side to side. "I didn't know it was your favorite. I was going to give it back, but then you and your friends gave me this look like you wished I'd get sucked into another universe. So I left."

"That's because you signed my book with *'Have a great summer, Melissa,'* with two *S*'s, like you didn't even know my name! Or didn't care."

"I did care! I just didn't know what to write. I'd signed a lot of yearbooks that day." She looked down and then up, with big, sad puppy eyes.

"Really?" I tilted my head, rubbing my thumb and finger together to play a tiny violin. Roxy had *so* many fans she just couldn't keep up with them. "Oh no. I feel so bad for you," I said flatly.

She gasped. She started saying something but instead of words, only random syllables came out until finally she giggled. I blinked. Had I heard that right? I couldn't help it. I started laughing too.

"Melissssa!" Roxy said, with extra *S*'s. "I promise I'll get you a new purple pen!"

"It was my favorite!" I teased, super dramatically. It had bothered me for so long, but now that I'd said it out loud, it seemed silly. Especially after everything Roxy and I had been through. "JMJ was so extra to you. I'm sorry!"

"Omg. I'm so sorry too!" Roxy fanned her face and tried to be serious, but that only made things funnier. "I can't believe I did that. Well, maybe I can. That was *totally* my brain goblin making things worse!"

"Wait, your what?"

Roxy got real quiet then and cleared the laughter from her throat. "Oh. It's just a thing my dad and I say sometimes."

Was it? I'd never heard Carlos use it. Maybe it was a just-between-them thing, like how no one but Papi called me Meli-Meli. Whatever it was, it seemed to have formed some sort of protective layer over Roxy, thicker than my own back brace.

"Anyway, Dad said you went to the fair," she said. "Did they have bottles of SPF sunscreen everywhere?"

I smiled at Roxy bringing up her old joke, and soon enough we were whispering under the covers, trying to keep from laughing too loud as we shared the day's funniest moments, like when Roxy and her friends nearly fell off the boat, or when James said that Pharaoh's Fury should be called Corn Dog's Revenge.

"That's clever. I didn't know James was so funny," Roxy said.

"He's just shy at first, before you get to know

him. Not a loud type like Lucia and Camila," I said. Roxy's grin plopped off her face like a fallen coconut. "Oh, no. I didn't mean that in a bad way, just that your friends are great! For you, you know?"

But there was no taking back what I'd said. Roxy sat up, pushing the covers away.

That was so much less judgy in my brain! I thought.

"It's fine. I get it," Roxy said.

"No! I just meant, I'm glad you saw them today. Because you must've missed them. Like I missed my friends. That's all."

Roxy let out a small huff and shook her head slowly. "Yup. I missed them a lot. You're right about that."

Somehow, though, it didn't feel right. It felt like only half the truth. "I missed—"

"You know, we better get to sleep," she cut in. "Dad dropped off the wedding invitations today, so tomorrow's a Big Disaster Day."

Before I could say anything more, she was at the bathroom doorway, leaving my room. As she flipped off the light, I noticed she was wearing two rings, the type that changed colors according to your mood. They were both black.

You'd think painting day would've been fun for me, but the next day, I had one goal only. I didn't say a word when Mami showed us the boring greige shade she and Roxy had chosen for the living room. I didn't even complain when our parents accidentally bought two gallons of the same guava pink for our rooms, instead of the very distinct ones we'd picked out: Coral Sunset and Fruit Punch.

What did it matter? The only thing I could focus on was getting Mami and Carlos to see that living together was chaos before everyone RSVP'd to the wedding. Last night had been all the proof we needed. If even after a day apart Roxy and I could still manage to hurt each other, what would a whole lifetime of sisterhood be like?

I reminded myself of James and Janette's advice: Commit. Take risks. If this next plan worked, the Floreses and Romeros would be out of this house before the paint dried. But that was a big *if*.

"We have to be super careful," I explained to Roxy. "If they suspect we did any of this on purpose, we're toast."

"I get it." She popped a stick of gum in her mouth but didn't offer me one. I noticed she was only wearing one ring instead of two. "The placement of the fan and the newspapers are crucial. They have to think it was all an accident. You've explained it like twenty-four times."

She rubbed her hand over a strip of blue painter's tape she'd laid over the baseboards in our rooms, just like Carlos had showed us.

"That's because you weren't listening for the first twenty-three."

"Sorry if my paying-attention-face doesn't look the same as yours. Some of us multitask."

"Are you saying I can't?"

"I'm saying we should just get started already."

So we did. We taped several rows of newspapers to the baseboard to cover the carpet. Unlike most things in this house, our parents wanted to keep it. They said it was brand new, and not having to redo the floors meant they could use that money for a really nice wedding photographer. But if Roxy and I did these rooms right, there'd soon be no wedding to photograph.

"Be careful! No gaps in the tape," I reminded her.

"I get it!"

It took forever, but we finally started painting. Roxy traced all the edges in our bedrooms with a wide brush, and I took a roller up and down the walls. It felt like we were working on a giant coloring book: she worked on the outlines, I colored them in. The newspapers we'd laid to protect the carpet from the paint crunched under our feet as we moved.

Every once in a while, Mami and Carlos would check on our progress. "It's looking so good, girls. You make an amazing team!" Carlos said.

Roxy and I smiled at each other, but not because we were happy. Because we knew the mayhem that was coming next.

"I can already imagine your dad trying to let us off the hook when he sees what we did here," I whispered as our parents headed back to the Bens' room.

They were busy trying to build a bunk bed they'd bought from IKEA. "He's probably gonna be all, 'They did their best, it's not their fault.'" I flung my arms around like a Muppet.

"Well, your mom's gonna be like, 'They're punished! Stick them in the attic with the bats for a month!'" She put one hand on her hip and another on her creased forehead, imitating Mami a little too well.

"Whatever. As long as it makes them call off the wedding."

"Exactly. Let's do my room first," Roxy said. She stood on one of the newspapers, then twisted her left foot, causing it to rip on purpose.

Using a wet brush, I let the paint splatter over the tear. To be extra thorough, Roxy widened the rip in the paper with one finger and I let the paint drip right on top of the carpet. A pink spot the size of a quarter oozed into the fibers, and then we set the newspaper back over it.

"Give it another splash," Roxy whispered. "To cover up the tear."

"I know. This was my idea, remember?"

"I'm just trying to help."

"Help? Or control everything?" I said.

She rolled her eyes. "Let's just be done with it."

We did the same paint splatter routine along the entire perimeter of both our rooms. Over and over, we let paint "accidentally" drip under the newspapers, until there was more paint on the carpet than the actual walls. When we were done, I couldn't help noticing that the messy newspapers actually looked beautiful, with the swirls and dots of paint making shapes like fireworks and spiderwebs.

"It reminds me of a Jackson Pollock," Roxy said.

"*You* know Pollock?"

"Shocker, right? My mom read a whole book about him. Years ago."

I couldn't imagine Roxy and her mom talking about art. I couldn't imagine them doing much of anything, because Roxy barely spoke about her. "Did your mom ever teach you to paint? If she were my mom, I would've—"

"Well, she's not," Roxy cut in. "And Evy isn't

mine. That's the whole point of this, remember?"

How could I forget? All I'd done was ask an innocent question and Roxy had snapped at me harder than a turtle in a canal. "Let's just wrap this up," I said. We needed to add the finishing touch to our scheme before the paint started to dry.

Carlos had taken a fan out for us, saying, "Turn it on when you're done to help things dry faster."

In the hallway, Mami had left a bunch of my things for me to unpack. Among them was a box of an antique teacup set Abuela had given me when I was three. It was fragile, so she'd used packing peanuts to protect it. The tiny bits of light Styrofoam were exactly what we needed.

We placed the teacup box with the packing peanuts in front of the fan.

"Ready?" Roxy said. I nodded and she flipped the switch.

CHAPTER 12
ROXY

The packing peanuts floated in the air, then, one by one, they attached themselves to the wet paint on the walls and floor, like confetti after the Super Bowl. Thousands of them covered every inch of both our bedrooms. It would take forever to pick them off, and then the rooms would have to be painted again. As for the carpet, it was a goner.

"Disastrous," I whispered to Meli. A few of the peanuts clung to her braids.

"It's sort of beautiful, actually." She turned her head from side to side as she watched the Styrofoam flutter and stick.

"That must be the artist in you," I said. "The most

important thing is that Evy and Dad are going to freak out."

Meli crossed her fingers, then the two of us went downstairs, leaving the fan and packing peanuts to do their worst. The boys were helping Dad build shelves for the garage, and Evy was in the living room, organizing the bookshelves. When she spotted us, she asked, "All done, girls?"

"Sí, Mami," Meli answered for us both.

"Bravo!" Evy cheered. She reached out, plucked a packing peanut from Meli's hair, and frowned.

I held my breath. Evy dropped the peanut into a trash bag on the ground. Saved!

"You've earned a break," Evy said. "Why don't you go get yourselves an ice cream at the park? Money's in the drawer under the microwave. Be back by five, por fa!" Then she wiped her brow and went back to work. Evy had been going nonstop for days. Dad, too. Even the boys were tired from all the work, but they were happy to be together.

Here Evy was, so happy and relieved that we'd tackled a big job, and she was rewarding us with ice cream. Every part of me wanted to rush upstairs and start taking down all those packing peanuts.

Meli must have sensed it, because she grabbed my wrist and said, "Steady." Like a coach would when a player got nervous. Without another word, we got the money and left the house. I didn't breathe until we were outside, then I let it all out at once.

"You okay, Roxy?" Meli asked.

"Nope. Not okay. Our parents are going to lose it when they see what we did!"

"Shh! Carlos will hear you." Meli pointed to the garage with her lips. "Listen," she said softly. "*We* weren't the ones who left that box with the packing peanuts out in the hall. And it wasn't *our* idea to turn on the fan. Get it?"

"I know that, Meli. But *we* are the ones who put those two things together. On purpose."

Now Meli had her hands on her hips, and maybe she was thinking about how her papi canceled her Legoland trip, or how peaceful it was in her old house and how much her friends hated me, but I don't think I'd ever seen her this determined.

"Yes, on purpose, because we *have* a purpose. A goal. A wish to get our lives back and this is how we do it. You said we needed to be relentless, didn't you?" I nodded. "Okay then. Let's go get our ice cream, and hopefully by the time we get back, everything will be right again."

The park was two blocks away, with a giant oak tree at its center. There was a place for dogs to run, a little stream to walk in, plastic playground equipment, a swing set, and an ice cream truck playing music parked out front. Meli ordered a Push-Up Pop and I got a snow cone. Then we sat down on the swings to enjoy our treats.

I wondered what was happening back at the house. Had Evy and Dad discovered our mess yet? I imagined the walls all covered in white and the fan hardening the paint with each passing minute. The longer it took to discover, the worse it would be.

That nervous feeling started up again, like a clock ticking *doom, doom, doom* in my head and stomach. Maybe we could still make it right. We could go back, stop the fan, tell our parents what happened, and offer to clean it all up. Maybe then that sick, anxious feeling would go away.

A little kid screamed, crouching on the ground at the edge of the park.

Meli and I took one look at each other and started running.

"Are you okay?" Meli shouted, running faster than me. Who knew Meli could *bolt* like that? We reached a little girl, about seven years old, hunched in front of a storm drain against the sidewalk.

"Misu!" the girl wailed and pointed into the dark mouth of the drain.

"What's a Misu?" Meli asked.

"Shh. Listen," I said. Then we heard it—a teeny-tiny, pitiful meow, followed by a splash and a gurgle. Then silence again.

"Misu's my kitten!" the girl cried. "She jumped out of my arms and ran in . . . in . . . there!" Her face was puffy and red, and she was doing that hiccup thing little kids do when they cry too hard and can't catch their breath anymore. We heard Misu meow again, weaker this time. It had rained earlier in the day, and the storm drain was full.

"That cat is drowning!" I said, panicking.

"Don't talk nonsense," Meli told me, then cut her eyes at the little girl in an expression that warned, *Be cool*. Meli was right. I had to calm down.

"We'll get Misu out," I assured the girl, even though I didn't believe it myself. "What's your name?"

"O-O-Ofelia," she said, crying a little less now that we were there. Meanwhile, Meli had flopped down on her stomach and was starting to wiggle herself *into* the storm drain, headfirst!

"Meli! Your back. Be careful."

"I will be! Just hold my legs." The girl and I each grabbed one of Meli's ankles and held on for life. Meli's head and shoulders were in the drain, and she was reaching down with both arms, trying to feel for the kitten.

"Come on, come on, Misu," we could hear Meli saying, her voice echoing in the darkness. Every once in a while, Misu would respond with a microscopic meow. I saw a big, fat cockroach crawl out of the storm drain, just an inch above Meli's head, but I kept my cool and didn't say a word. After a few tense moments, Meli shouted, "Got her!" She reached behind her back and dropped a dripping orange kitten with a blue ribbon around its neck at our feet.

"Misu, Misu, Misu!" Ofelia shouted, hugging the drenched cat, who blinked in the sunlight and clawed at Ofelia's arms. "You saved her!"

"Her?" I asked. "Misu must be really special. Most orange cats are male. Did you know that?"

Ofelia shook her head, then snuggled her super-special cat some more. I felt really proud just then.

Meli, meanwhile, was still halfway down the drain. "Meli, you're a hero!" I said, wiggling her ankle.

"Stuck."

"What?" I wiggled her ankle some more.

"I'm stuck, Roxy. I'm stuck! Pull! Pull! Ow. Not so hard."

I rocked Meli side to side, like we were in a wheelbarrow race. Slowly, she emerged from the storm drain, her shirt soaked, and her arms crisscrossed with cat scratches.

Meli sat down against the curb like a sack of potatoes and blew out a big puff of air.

I secretly checked her hair for cockroaches and was relieved none of them had hitched a ride.

"What? What is it?" she said, frantically patting down her head.

"Nothing, but, um, what if you get ringworm?" I asked, pointing at her arms.

Meli took one look at me, grabbed my hands, and laughed. "Tell that goblin in your brain to be quiet, huh? We just saved a life!"

We both looked at Ofelia and Misu, who were now cuddling on a patch of grass a few feet away. "Yeah, we did that."

Meli and I were still holding hands when my phone pinged. I pulled it out of my pocket and there was a text from Dad.

ROXANA, COME HOME. RIGHT NOW.

Oh no.

"Meli, they know. Check your phone."

Meli's face lost all its color at once. She slipped her phone out from her crossbody purse and checked her messages. I could tell from the way her eyebrows jumped that Evy had texted her too.

This was it. Somehow they'd realized we set the whole thing up. Dad would probably take my phone, pull me from the flag football team, and never buy my favorite cereal again. As for Evy, she'd probably send Meli away. Maybe all the way to Peru.

"We need to go home," she said. I nodded, helping Meli get on her feet. We walked slowly out of the park, like we were on our way to the principal's office but ten times worse. Ofelia and Misu looked up at us as we passed them.

"Misu says thank you," Ofelia called.

"You're welcome, Misu," Meli and I answered together.

"I wish I had a sister," I heard Ofelia say to her cat. I wondered if Meli had heard it too. I wondered if it made her heart hurt like it did mine.

We were almost home when Meli started sniffing and wiping away tears with her free hand.

"Hey, are you okay?"

Meli shook her head.

There was something I wanted to say but it would take a lot of courage. So I took a deep breath, told the goblin to shush, and spoke slowly and softly. "When I was little, I used to wish for a sister all the time. I wished for one every time I threw a penny into a fountain or caught an eyelash on my fingertip. But when my dad started dating your mom, a sister was the last thing I wanted. I was Dad's girl. Me. You still have your papi to yourself. I have to share my dad with you. You get it?"

Meli nodded. "I get it. I hate the idea of sharing my mom with you. I was la niña de mamá. Now she has two niñas."

"Had," I said.

"Had," Meli agreed. "Roxy, sometimes you make me feel like I'm some nerd who isn't worth your time."

"And you're always interrupting me as if I'm just not as smart as you are," I added.

We walked on quietly, more slowly than before. In some ways, we'd been having the same argument over and over again—Meli thinking I was thoughtless, and me thinking she was judgmental. All I ever wanted was for her to say, "I'm sorry, Roxy. I know how you feel." Maybe that's all Meli wanted too.

So I said it, right there on the sidewalk.

"I'm sorry about all of it," I told her. "Especially for all the mean thoughts I ever had about you. I'm sorry, Meli. And if we can't be family, then I want us to be friends."

Meli wiped her cheeks, then took my hands. "Sorry, they're wet," she said, then added, "I used to think all you wanted was to be the center of attention, but I'm realizing now that maybe you were just trying to cheer me up."

"Yeah, but sometimes I made things worse, didn't I?"

"Maybe, but I could loosen up sometimes too."

She let go of my hands. "I think we might have messed up. Bad."

"Well," I said, "if you're going to get yourself into a pickle, be ready for things to turn sour. At least that's what Dad always says."

Meli nodded. "I hate pickles. All this time we've tried to stop our families from coming together, but maybe we were wrong. Maybe we really were meant to be—"

"Sisters," we said together.

Meli nodded and wiped her cheeks dry again. For the first time since the start of the summer, something felt . . . right.

"But look, Roxy, it's too late." She raised her phone and showed me the text from her mom:

COME HOME, PLEASE, WE NEED TO GO.

Part Three:
All ~~Mixed~~ Fixed Up?

CHAPTER 13
MELI

The sun was scorching by the time we got back to the house, but when we walked inside, it was ice-cold. Not just in the air, but in my veins. I got that horrible, chilly feeling I used to get when Mami and Papi would fight all the time. Except now it was coming from Carlos and Mami.

"Oh good, you're back," Mami said, barely looking at me as she piled all our stuff by the entrance. There were Benji's and my sleeping bags, an opened box labeled TOILETRIES that actually had a bunch of our clothes in it, and mom's pink hardshell carry-on suitcase.

"Where are we going?" My voice shook.

"To your— Meli, what happened to your arms?!" She dropped two pillows on the couch as she rushed over to examine the marks Misu had left.

"It's not as bad as it looks!" The scratches were red and bumpy, but the blood was already drying, and my arms itched more than they hurt. "There was this cat, and Roxy and I—"

"No me digas! Let me guess, you and Roxy were fighting again."

"No! Honest!" Roxy said, but Mami held up one hand for us to be quiet.

"I can't take any more chaos today, girls. Por fa. Just bring me the bandages so we can get you cleaned up, and we'll talk about this when we get to Abuela's."

"Abuela's?"

Mami gave me a look, the kind that warned *not now*.

"I'll get the first aid kit!" Roxy said, dashing nervously out of the living room. While we waited, Mami resumed packing soaps, packs of tissues, and snacks from the pantry, but Carlos just stood by the kitchen island, nibbling on his thumbnail. It was the first time he wasn't rushing to help Mami when she had her hands full.

Roxy came back holding a box of bandages, a bottle of hydrogen peroxide, and a bag of cotton balls. "Let me do it. I already washed my hands." We sat on the floor while she dabbed at my wounds. "Does that hurt?"

I winced and nodded. My hands started to shake, but Roxy's were steady, strong like her grip had been while I hung over the edge of the storm drain. I couldn't believe I'd actually done that. *We'd* actually done that. It'd happened fast, but replaying it now in my mind I realized I would've never jumped into that drain hole if Roxy hadn't had my back. Deep in my gut, I'd known I could trust her. I'd known with a certainty I'd hadn't felt in months that Roxy wouldn't let me down.

"I'm sorry, Meli," she said, eyeing the duffel bag that Mami had just placed at the door.

Carlos walked over to me with his hands in his pockets. "You okay, kiddo?" It was the first time he'd ever called me that. I couldn't believe it would probably be the last.

I stood up, shaking my head. "No. I don't want to go. I don't want any of us to go."

"Me neither." Roxy took a box from Mami and walked it back across the living room into the hall. She smiled like everything was fine, but I could see the edge of her lips tremble. "We're almost done fixing the house. Right?"

"No, querida, Roxy. Not everything can be fixed." Mami's voice was sad and gentle.

"Daddy? What's going on?"

Maybe the fear in Roxy's voice did something to him, because Carlos stood up straighter, like a switch had gone off inside him, and moved closer to Roxy to place his hand on her shoulder. "Nothing bad, Rox. It just turns out this house has some pretty big issues we didn't see right away. It happens sometimes."

"Exactly. There's, uh . . . foundational problems," Mami added.

"Oversights, really. I wouldn't use the word *problems*," Carlos said.

"Ah, semantics." Mami grinned. But not once did they look at each other as they spoke.

Carlos grew serious. "I saw your list, Evy."

"What list?" I cut in. I thought they'd fought because of our rooms, but was something else going on?

"No interrumpas, Meli. It's nothing," Mami said. Her eyes grew wide as she finally met Carlos's. "And you still want to do this?" She tilted her head at the door.

Carlos nodded, then he left the room.

Mami loved lists. To-do lists everywhere! But there was no way this particular list was "nothing." In fact, it seemed like a very big, very bad *something*. They were trying to hide the truth from us, but adults aren't as good at keeping secrets as they think they are. One quick glance at Mami's hand confirmed my suspicions.

No engagement ring!

"Meli?" Roxy must've noticed it too. Her eyes filled to the brim as they met mine.

One more second of this and I knew we'd both cry big, ugly tears.

"I, uh . . . I left something in our room!" I said, signaling for Roxy to follow me up the stairs.

"*Our* room?" she whispered.

"It slipped out," I said. We'd spent so much time painting and scheming in both rooms, I'd started thinking of them as one space. Roxy and Meli's. Ours.

But then we stepped inside.

"Oh. Em. Cheez-Its," Roxy said.

"I have no words."

When we'd set the packing peanuts soaring, we never predicted this. Not only had they stuck to the wall, but about half of them had fallen onto the sopping wet paint carpet. Pink footprints half the size of our feet left a squiggly-lined trail all through the bathroom.

"The Benjamins!" we said at once.

"Do you think they got in trouble?" I asked.

Roxy nodded, then started shaking her head side to side. "Maybe our parents got mad at us, and then at them, and then each other . . ."

"Oh no." I looked around the room. Between the paint and the green peanuts and the black-and-white newspapers, it was a nightmare. "It looks like Beetlejuice's house in here."

"Speaking of houses, looks like we won't be living in this one together after all," Roxy said. "We have to *do* something! Think!"

But all I could think about was when we saved Misu. The rush of doing something so completely unlike me, yet still having it feel right. All this time I'd been missing my old life, wanting things to feel familiar again. I hadn't stopped to imagine that this new life being Roxy's sister could be full of surprises. When it really mattered, we'd been brave and heroic together. We'd made each other strong. I'd been so scared when Roxy came into my life: scared of losing Mami and Papi, scared of being away from my friends, scared of missing home. In that storm drain, though, I'd felt I could face any fear so long as she and I did it together.

And now we were being torn apart. "We would've made a really cool family," I finally said.

From downstairs, I heard Mami yell that I had ten seconds to get in the car.

Roxy stood in front of the bedroom door. "No! Don't give up. Not yet."

I looked at her arms spread wide, blocking the way. I did the only thing I could. I hugged her.

"This is all your fault," Benji said as we climbed into the car. His eyes were red and puffy, dried snot clinging to his nose. He and Ben had said goodbye in the driveway, throwing a tantrum epic enough for our next-door neighbors to hear. Roxy and I were more private, I guess. We just held hands until it was time to let go.

"Text me when you get there?" she said.

"Promise."

My abuela's town house was a short drive away, in a retirement community that had a year-round heated pool and a banquet hall where she and her friends played dominoes every Sunday. Mis viejitas, she called them, which was funny because they were as old as she was. Abuela was always saying she couldn't believe it took sixty years for her to meet her best friends, and now she couldn't imagine living without them. As I clipped on my seat belt, I finally understood what she meant. Roxy and I had spent all this time being frenemies, and now I couldn't stand the thought of not being sisters.

I *had* to think of a plan to keep Mami from pulling out of the driveway, but my mind was blank. It wasn't fair. Why had it been so easy to think of ways to break her and Carlos up? Why was it so hard now to make them get back together? And what list were they talking about?

Through the windshield, I watched as they said their last goodbye. It was nothing more than a stiff, awkward air kiss, the kind adults give when they're just being polite. I looked away.

"Benji?"

"I'm not talking to you."

"Benji, this is important. You have to tell me what happened between them while Roxy and I were at the park!"

"I don't know!" He crossed his arms. "It all started in your rooms and got bad from there. Mami was like, 'Don't blame Meli.' And then Carlos said, 'Well, don't blame Roxy.' And then we heard a bunch of noise in the kitchen until they went into their room and shut the door, but Ben and I pressed a plastic cup against it to listen and then Carlos said something about Mami taking things too seriously and she said, 'Well, you're never serious enough!'" Benji was breathing real deep now, on the verge of tears again. "It was bad, Meli."

"I'm so sorry," I said, just as Mami climbed in next to me.

"¿Que? Oh hijita, don't be. I should be the one apologizing to you. Both of you. We rushed into things. We were just so excited when we saw the house and then—" Mami grew quiet as she put the car in reverse and the house—as well as Roxy, Carlos, and Ben—got further and further away. We stopped at a red light next to the park where it seemed like only seconds ago I'd realized Roxy was family. In a blink I had lost her.

My phone dinged in my pocket. It was a selfie of

Papi at an airport, telling me he was headed to Peru next for his documentary. *Almost done,* he wrote. *And soon we can go to Legoland after all!*

Can't wait, I wrote back. But it didn't really feel like Legoland mattered anymore.

Neither Mami, Benji, or I had much of an appetite by the time we got to Abuela's house, so instead of dinner she made us lonchecito: toast and jam with café con leche for Mami, and hot chocolate for us kids. I finished mine quickly and sat on the kitchen floor with Kiwi, who curled up in a ball on my lap. Benji went to take a nap on the couch.

"Good girl, Kiwi. You comfort Meli while I comfort Evy," Abuela said. She poured Mami more coffee and sighed. "I'm proud of you, hija. You followed your heart. It doesn't always work out the way you think. But you tried."

"And now what?" Mami said.

"Now you have a home here, always. Or at least until you get tired of me."

They both chuckled quietly, but I didn't see what was so funny. I loved Abuela, but living with her? She snored at night, and Kiwi farted silent but deadlies. And if we stayed here, I wouldn't see Roxy again until school started.

I wished I didn't miss her this much already. I wished I could make us move back in with the Romeros. But I couldn't, so I wished I could go back in time and make it so our parents never fell in love in the first place.

"Mami?" I'd just thought of something.

"Hmm?"

"What was the list Carlos mentioned?"

Mami looked away. "Nada, Meli."

There it was again—Mami and Carlos's big, secret "nothing." I hated to think she didn't trust me, but how could she after everything Roxy and I had pulled?

"I'm sorry for the mess we made painting our rooms, Mami. We didn't mean to cause so much trouble."

But that was a lie. We'd totally meant to cause all that trouble. We just didn't know we'd hurt everyone in the process.

"Is that what you think this is about? Oh, Meli. That's not what happened."

"Then what? Why did we leave? And why aren't you wearing your ring?"

Mami covered her hand as if she was surprised I'd noticed. "It's . . . complicated."

"You always say that! Try me, for once. I'm old enough."

The adults exchanged looks. Abuela gave Mami her *cuidado* stare.

"Well . . . we did get upset about the paint. But only because it confirmed something I'd been worried about for a while: we're too different. You and Benji and I, we're used to certain routines, structure. And Carlos, well . . . he lets his kids run wild. I mean, look what happened to your arms at the park! Our families are opposites, and not in a good way."

"That's not true! The Bens are best friends. And Roxy and I are actually pretty great together. And the house is almost done!"

"Ay, hijita. It's so far from done. In fact, it's worse now because I got so frustrated arguing with Carlos that I tripped over the box of tiles for the kitchen backsplash. And they all broke into a million pieces! Shattered everywhere." Mami stretched out one arm for emphasis, and I gasped, thinking about all those bright colors. They would've looked so pretty in the kitchen. For the first time since all this started, I imagined us really living there: Roxy and I doing homework together on the kitchen island. Mami helping Carlos make picnic dinner on a weeknight while the Bens played whatever new card game they'd made up. It could've really been a happy home.

"Maybe we can fix the tiles. Roxy and I can glue them back together." I was pulling at straws now, whining worse than Benji, but I'd run out of plans and schemes.

Mami took the last sip of her coffee and shook her head. "I'm sorry, Meli. Sometimes you can't fix what's broken."

CHAPTER 14
ROXY

Dad booked a hotel a mile from the house for the night. As soon as Evy, Meli, and Benji left, we got into our car and headed out.

The only sound as we pulled out of the driveway was the gearshift as Dad pushed it forcefully. Finally, he spoke up. "Rox, be honest. Those scratches on Meli's arms—"

"—were from a kitten! Dad! I'd never hurt Meli. Never, ever!" Tears sprung into my eyes. Did Dad and Evy really think that I would ever—

"I believe you," Dad said, interrupting my thoughts and reaching out to pat my knee. "But I had to ask."

Did he have to ask? Had Meli and I fought *that* much? I closed my eyes and started rehearsing how I was going to explain all of this to Dr. Nordan when I saw her again for my next appointment. I didn't need Dr. Nordan to tell me what I realized was true. By putting our Disaster Plan into action instead of being honest with our parents, we had made everyone miserable. We'd told ourselves that what we were doing was helping everyone—was getting us back to *normal*—but really we were just being selfish.

"Why couldn't we stay in the house?" Ben asked from the back seat. Dad shook his head but didn't answer.

"The hotel has a pool," Dad said after a while, trying to be cheerful.

"Our old house had a pool," I said. "I mean, it's sort of green and all. But still."

"And a trampoline. And my brother, Benji," Ben shouted from the back seat. He'd been furious—slamming the car door, kicking the back of Dad's seat. It took me by surprise. Ben was usually calm as a lake, and just as deep. Dad must have been surprised, too, because he didn't tell Ben to behave.

"Listen, bud," Dad started to say, "forming a blended family is a huge step. Evy and I rushed things and put all you kids through too much too soon."

Ben kicked Dad's seat again, this time with both feet. "I liked being in a blender! Benji and I were a delicious smoothie!"

Before Dad could say anything about smoothies, delicious or otherwise, I cut in. "I don't want us all to break up. Meli and I were working things out, like sisters," I pleaded. Dad didn't say anything, but I could see a muscle in his jaw flexing, like he was trying to stop himself from talking. Or crying.

Before I knew it, we were at the hotel. Dad put the car in park and said, "Things are going to get back to normal now." Then he got out and started unpacking our bags.

Back to normal. Isn't that what I'd wanted all summer long? Me, Ben, and Dad could be a unit again. I wouldn't have to share Dad with two other kids who didn't always get us or the way we did things.

I wouldn't have to eat Evy's healthy snacks, or stay quiet while Meli did her yoga, or live by all their rigid rules.

Also, I wouldn't have to explain my mom to them—her retreat to New Jersey, her depression. In fact, I wouldn't have to talk to anyone about her, or the times it just crushed me.

I could go back to the way I was. I could keep all those big feelings just between me, Dad, and Dr. Nordan.

Forever.

But wasn't that the whole point of having a family? Not needing to carry all the hard parts of life on your own? It was nice sharing my feelings with Meli. And I bet Evy and Benji were good listeners too.

I grabbed my suitcase and tried to quiet my mind in the lobby while Dad got our key. Ben was still mad and yanked his suitcase handle so hard it snapped. Once again, Dad didn't say anything, but Ben had to carry his bag with both arms. Finally, we reached our suite. There was a bedroom for Dad and one for me and Ben to share. I think Dad must have wanted a space to be alone, because he went directly to his bedroom and closed the door, which left me and Ben alone in the living room.

Ben sat on the sofa, drew his legs up, and rested his forehead on his knees. He looked so small and pitiful. I sat beside him. "Ben, I'm so sorry."

"For what? This is all Dad's fault," he mumbled into his knees.

"What do you mean, 'It's Dad's fault'?"

Ben lowered his voice to a whisper. "When Dad and Evy saw the mess upstairs, they started fighting. Evy started to cry, then Dad said it was all an accident. Then Evy said, 'This is no accident, Carlos!' THEN Dad said, 'Why do you always blame the kids? You're too hard on them.' AND THEN Evy said—"

I put my hand on Ben's mouth to keep him from saying more. I could imagine the rest. Evy and Dad clashing over how to deal with me and Meli.

I took a big, steadying breath. "It's not Dad's fault. Or Evy's." Then I told him everything—how Meli and I couldn't get along, how we came up with the Disaster Plan, and how we realized, too late, that we really were a family and wanted to stay that way.

Ben raised his head at last and his eyes were full of tears. "I'm so mad at you," he whispered.

"I deserve that."

"But you and Meli were pretty sneaky, I gotta say." Dad's cell phone rang. We heard him talking with somebody but couldn't make out what he was saying. I hoped it was Evy. I hoped they were patching things up.

"Meli and I made a good team," I said.

"A delicious smoothie, like me and Benji."

I imagined all of us swimming in a big pool full of milk and fruit, with globs of whipped cream—like hats on our heads, which made me laugh.

"What's so funny?" Ben asked.

"Nothing," I lied. There was no way I could explain that visual and not sound completely bananas. I started tickling him, which usually helped to get him out of a sad mood. But this time, it backfired.

"Quit it!" Ben said, shoving me hard. "You and Meli ruined everything."

I pushed him back. "We were trying to go back

to the way things were before. But we realized it was wrong."

Ben's nostrils flared. He pinched my arm. "You realized TOO LATE."

My arm throbbed, and a big ball of anger formed in my chest. I couldn't help it. "Don't DO that!" I shouted, pinching Ben's arm back. In a flash, he jumped at me, and soon the two of us were rolling around on the carpet, getting pinches in. Deep down, I wasn't mad at Ben. And I don't think he was mad at me.

"Hey, guys. Guys! GUYS!" We stopped mid-wrestle. Dad was at the doorway of his room. His eyes were red. He looked miserable, so different from the way he looked when Evy was around. He had a hotel blanket rolled up under his arm. "Let's get some fresh air."

On any other day, pulling up to the parking lot of the Miami Dolphins' training camp would've felt like every holiday and birthday rolled into one.

But this time felt like pretending the skies were blue and sunny during a hurricane.

Ben and I followed Dad up a grassy berm overlooking the field where the Dolphins were practicing. We had a good view, and as we laid out the hotel blanket, we could hear the coaches and players shouting about plays. Ben got comfy on his stomach, his chin resting on his hands. Dad sat cross-legged and I knelt beside him.

"The QB looks good this year," he said.

"He makes it look easy."

"Hard things only look easy if you work your tail off." We watched as the quarterback leaned back and threw long into the hands of the receiver. Dad put his arm around my shoulder and I leaned in and smelled his cologne. The sun was baking but the berm was in the shade, and it wasn't too hot.

Beside us, Ben put his head down and closed his eyes. He probably should have brought a book to entertain himself.

"Speaking of hard things," Dad began. "How are

you doing? We haven't been to the talking doctor in a while."

"That's true," I said just as the wide receiver chewed up a few more yards.

One of the safeties was yelling, "Sun's out, squad's out!" so loudly we could hear it on the hill.

Dad had brought a lunchbox with us. He'd packed chips and juice boxes. "Here you go," he said, handing me one of each. "So, what do you think? Do we have a good team this year?"

I didn't answer him. Who cared about football at a time like this? Our family had fallen apart, but we were talking about the next season?

The quarterback sent the ball flying into the red zone and teammates were shouting, "Lock it in! Lock it in!" It felt like they were talking to me.

So I zeroed in on the goal.

I waited until Dad had put a handful of chips in his mouth so that he wouldn't answer right away, then I said, "Meli and Benji feel like family. And Evy too. Please make up with her. Please."

He chewed slowly, looking down at his lap the

whole time, looking like a player who knew he'd already lost the game. "It's a lot more complicated than that, kiddo."

"Please, Dad." I wanted to keep saying it—please, please, please—until Dad finally gave in. But I held my tongue.

"Roxy, I don't have a Hail Mary pass left in me, you understand?"

I nodded. Sometimes there was no coming back from a losing score.

Dr. Nordan always said that anxiety goblins like mine got bigger in the face of uncertainty, and I could hear it whispering to me now, demanding answers.

Say 'please' again, Rox. Say it ten million more times. Tell him about the Disaster Plan. Tell him that if he doesn't make up with Evy, that you'll quit football and school and will never eat another vegetable for as long as you live.

Shh, I said in return. *I'll be okay, no matter what. This stinks, that's all.*

Dad let out a long breath. "Let's just watch the rest of practice, then we can have dinner. We'll let Ben pick the restaurant."

I looked over at my brother, who was snoring lightly. "Ugh. He always picks the Dino Diner." It was true; Ben couldn't pass up a chance to eat at the dinosaur restaurant at the mall, the one where the chicken nuggets were so rubbery they bounced.

"Dolphins practice for you, Dino joint for Ben. Fair's fair."

"Fair's fair," I repeated, even though nothing felt fair at all.

CHAPTER 15
MELI

Sleeping over at Abuela's house when I was little used to be nonstop fun—we'd do crafts together, make alfajores, and at night she'd act out bedtime stories of her childhood in Peru. But sleeping over at Abuela's house now that Mami and Carlos's wedding had been called off? It was Boringsville, population five. Mami took more naps than I'd ever seen her take in my life. Benji acted like I was invisible, and Abuela was too busy with her homeowner association meetings to cheer any of us up. Even Kiwi was acting strange, barely touching her food.

"Meli, why are you still in bed?! We can't be late for your appointment!" Mami rushed through the living room putting on her earrings, shoes, and lipstick. For three long days, life had been put on hold, but now it was time for my six-month checkup to see if my spine had kept curving.

I couldn't believe I'd almost forgotten about it. Before Mami and Carlos got engaged, the fear of my scoliosis progressing was constantly in the back of my mind. The Disaster Plan had distracted me from all of that, but the truth was, so had Roxy.

"I'll be quick!" I said, dashing from the sofa bed to the bathroom to take off my brace and get dressed. Dr. Moss's office wasn't that far away, and Mami's idea of being late still meant we'd be five minutes early. When we arrived, I sat next to the aquarium in the corner of the waiting room while Mami checked me in.

"How's it going, Shellory?" I whispered to the hermit crab I'd named the day of my first appointment. She was the one who'd inspired my sculpture for the talent show.

"So, how are James and Janette?" Mami said once she finished filling out several forms. She always tried to pass the time at my appointments by talking about anything *but* my spine.

I sighed. "I don't know. They don't get back from performing arts camp until tomorrow." All I'd heard from them were a bunch of *Congrats!* and *Yay!* memes after I'd texted them that our parents had split.

I think we made a mistake, I'd written back. *I miss Roxy.*

But by then I guess they'd turned off their cells.

I leaned my forehead against the glass. Shellory stuck out one arm and seemed to wave.

"You know, you and Shellory have a lot in common," Mami said.

"We do?"

"Hermit crabs live inside their seashells, where they feel protected. They keep all their soft feelings inside, behind a tough exterior. ¿Me entiendes, Meli?"

I nodded. I had done the same with Mami by not being honest about my emotions ever since she and Carlos got together.

"So when I ask you how you feel about something,

it's because I really want to know because I care about you. I had no idea until this summer that you and Roxy disliked each other so much."

"We don't! I mean, I thought we did, but then we worked it out and now we—"

"Melisa Flores?" A technician in white scrubs with pink and purple hearts called us into the examination room and handed me a paper gown. "When you're done changing, meet me across the hall so we can get your picture taken," she said cheerfully.

I'd gotten enough of these to know the "picture" was really an X-ray. In a dark room, I stood against a cold metal square while a giant, white crane-looking machine pointed a light at my spine. It was weird to think this contraption could see through me right down to my bones.

"Now don't move," she said, and I held my breath while it whirred to life. She did this two more times, and then Mami and I went back to the room to wait for Dr. Moss to show us the X-rays. I watched the clock, feeling like I was being graded on a test.

"Do you think the angle went up?" I finally asked.

That was how they measured the curve in my spine, like the degrees in a triangle.

Mami had been leafing through her planner, but now she set it down on her lap face up. "I don't know, hijita. But if it did, that won't mean it's your fault, or anyone's fault. We're doing our best, taking it one day at a time, okay?"

I nodded and glanced at the to-do list scribbled on her planner. In perfectly neat handwriting it said:

Find new real estate agent (not Carlos)

Hire movers again

View potential rentals

Email guests that wedding's off

As if that wasn't horrible enough, below it she'd written the addresses of three apartment buildings, all of them in a completely different neighborhood from this one. Janette's cousin lived there, and she didn't even go to our school!

"We're moving that far?!" I exclaimed.

"It's only fifteen minutes from here, and I've barely started looking," Mami said.

"But wouldn't I have to change schools?" I

asked, just as Dr. Moss came into the room.

Mami didn't answer me. Instead the three of us said hello and Dr. Moss asked me if I was having fun this summer, and all I could mumble was *It's been fine* until she pulled up my X-rays on her monitor. She dragged a mouse over the side by side images of my spine six months ago and now.

"The curve in your spine has gone up by two degrees, but your case is still in the mild range."

All I heard was *gone up*. My lip started to shake.

"It's just a tiny change," Dr. Moss reassured us.

Not a single change in my life felt tiny. Not one. "I wore my brace every night. And did all the yoga."

"You did great, Melisa. You probably kept that number from going up further. Which is why I'm not concerned at this point. Keep doing what you're doing, and we'll see where we're at in another six months."

After Dr. Moss left the room, Mami wrapped me in her arms. "That's great, Meli, you see? Nothing to worry about."

When would she finally understand? First it was

a curve of two degrees, then a house fifteen minutes away, then the wedding getting called off and Carlos and Mami never seeing each other again and a whole new school and life completely away from Roxy. As I changed back into my clothes I realized I was doing it again: going into my shell. As long as I hid behind it, Mami would never know what I was going through.

"It's just that all these tiny changes are a lot," I said. "And I'm scared. I wish we could go back to how it was, the six of us with the Romeros. I promise Roxy and I will get along. I don't want to lose her. She makes me feel brave."

"Ay, hijita. You and Roxy can still stay friends. Just because Carlos and I aren't, you know." She looked away and dabbed at her eye. "Our relationship doesn't change yours, is what I mean."

"But it does! Did you know she was helping me with my brace at night? And I was teaching her to do yoga. But now it won't be the same, and it's all our fault."

"No, Meli. You can't blame yourself. I promise, you and Roxy did nothing wrong. This whole situation with Carlos and me is about a lot more than just one fight." She put her notebooks and planners back into her purse as we left the room. I wished I could take an eraser to her lists and make all our problems go away.

Mami offered to stop for smoothies on the way back to Abuela's, but I wasn't in the mood. She didn't insist because she had a lot of errands to run. Apartment-hunting, I assumed. When we pulled into the driveway, she handed me a single key on a key chain. "Give this to your abuela, please. She'll know what to do with it."

I recognized the teal heart that hung on the chain. It was for the front door of the fixer-upper. Disappointment must've been written all over my face because Mami kissed me and said, "Tranquila. It's all going to be okay. You'll see."

I walked inside to the little *tap-tap-tap* of Kiwi's feet against the tile, and the saddest puppy eyes I'd ever seen.

"Great," I said. "I thought you were supposed to cheer people up, not the other way around."

"En español, por fa." Abuela came down the hall wearing purple workout pants and a yellow sweater. "You know Kiwi isn't bilingual."

"Okay, Kiwi. Ven conmigo." In the kitchen I gave her a biscuit from the treat jar and helped Abuela make lunch while she told me all about her packed day: an online Pilates class at two followed by an at-home massage, then a bite at a new food truck that one of her viejitas had just opened. It was official: my grandmother had a better social life than I did.

How'd the Dr's go? Roxy texted as I finished my meal. We'd been chatting back and forth for days but hadn't actually talked or FaceTimed, afraid our parents would overhear us.

Not bad. Not great. More wait and see.

Bummer.

Yeah. Wish I could get out of Boringsville.

She replied: Me too! The hotel pool is a puddle compared to our old one :(

On the bright side, Mami finally left the house! Can you get away?

I think so. But where?

Kiwi scratched at my leg and wagged her tail. "¡Que buena idea, Kiwi!"

Abuela was excited that I offered to take Kiwi for a walk, but Benji was ecstatic. When I whispered to him that we were meeting Roxy and Ben at the park he lit up like a video game character that suddenly got a full-life bar.

"Can you tell him to bring his race car? And the baseball gloves? And a baseball?" he whispered back.

I waited till we were on the sidewalk and out of earshot from Abuela. "I doubt they took all those things with them to the hotel," I said, thinking of everything we left behind at the house.

When we got to the park, I let Kiwi sniff around while Benji sat at a picnic table waiting for Roxy and Ben. A high-pitched *squeeee!* came up from behind me.

"Melimelimelimeliiiiii!" Roxy hugged me so hard I almost lost my balance, but I didn't care. "I thought we'd never get out of the hotel. Dad's got us doing all these games and activities, probably to distract himself from thinking about Evy. But you're here! And we made it!"

She was out of breath and red-faced, like she'd run over here, and she was so giddy it was contagious.

"I have so much to tell you!" I said.

We sat on a cement park bench that was curved like a half-moon. It was covered in splashes of multicolored tile, arranged in swirls like the waves of the ocean. We fell quiet.

The boys cackled as they teetered back and forth on the seesaw. "Look how happy they are," Roxy said. "They balance each other out. Literally. And we ruined it."

As if she agreed, Kiwi made a perfectly shaped poop emoji on the grass. "Real subtle, girl," I said, scooping it up with a doggie bag. "Muy sutil."

Roxy's foot tapped against the ground, practically vibrating. "We can't just sit here doing nothing! Think, Rox, think!"

I sighed and picked at my thumbnail. "Any minute now, Mami's going to tell all the guests that the wedding's toast."

"I know. Which means we have to act fast. Dad wants to sell the house ASAP. He says the housing market's fickle."

"What's fickle?" Benji asked. I hadn't noticed that the boys had stopped seesawing to listen in on our conversation.

"It means unpredictable. Something that can change at any moment." *Like our family,* I thought. "It's no use. Mami's made up her mind. I tried telling her we want to be together, but she won't lis—"

"But we have to keep trying," Ben said. "And we can't just talk. We have to *do*."

He was usually so quiet, the certainty in his voice caught me off guard.

"They don't believe we can be a family. So we have to show them," he said.

"Yeah!" Benji said. "Make them believe!"

Roxy and I exchanged glances.

"You know, our Disaster Plan only ruined our lives because technically it worked. Maybe *too* well . . . ," I said.

Roxy nodded in agreement. "All we need is a new

plan. No more Disaster Plan. We need a . . . a . . ."

"A BUILDING plan! So that we can rebuild our family!" Benji jumped onto the bench, his little body hovering over us. My stomach flipped in a good way, filling with hope.

"Okay, so what's step one?" I asked.

"No steps," Benji said, staring off in the direction of the fixer-upper. "This isn't levels one and two on a video game. This is the final boss level."

"Yeah! We go big," Ben said.

"Or we don't go home." Roxy raised her eyebrows in a mischievous, challenge-accepted kind of way.

I took a deep breath and looked at the bench beneath Benji's feet. Even with all the cracks that ran through it, it didn't wobble. It was solid. It made me think of my scoliosis sculpture and something Roxy had said the first time she saw all its cracks and holes. *It's still beautiful.* Little pieces of an idea started coming together in my mind.

"I think I've got it. But it means we'll have to get into the house alone. And keep our parents out of it."

"Well, that second part's easy. Dad says he wants to stay as far away as possible," Roxy said. "But the first . . ."

"Mami gave Abuela the key!" Benji shouted.

I checked the time on my phone. "Twenty minutes till her Pilates class starts. She doesn't like interruptions."

"You really think she'll give it to us?" Roxy asked.

"We have to try!" Ben reminded us.

We ran as fast as we could to Abuela's town house, and we arrived thirsty and out of breath, with Kiwi's tongue hanging halfway out of her head. Abuela had already started warming up for her workout, but she listened as we blurted out our whole plan, all of us at once in a jumbled mess of words.

"So . . . can we . . . have . . . the key?" Benji asked.

"Hmmm." She paced back and forth barefoot. "I don't think Evy would approve of you kids being alone in the house."

Roxy dropped her shoulders, and visions of Benji and me alone at a new school flashed before my eyes. Then Abuela folded her laptop shut as her workout video started streaming. We heard the tiniest jingle as she held up one hand to show us the key to the house.

"Bueno, pues. I guess we'll all just have to do this together."

CHAPTER 16
ROXY

"Ay Dios," Meli's abuela whispered when we showed her the mess we'd made.

"It's bad, huh?" Meli asked, and the rest of us nodded slowly. The paint on the carpet had semi-dried, so that it felt like mud underfoot, and the packing peanuts made the walls look like they'd broken out in a million pimples.

Ben and Benji went up to the walls and ran their hands over them. The packing peanuts fell off easily. Before anyone could say anything, Ben was carrying Benji on his shoulders, and they were wiping peanuts off the walls in big swoops.

"¡Así se hace!" Meli's abuela applauded. Meli and I pulled up the wet newspaper from the ground and rolled it up into a trash can. Carefully, we peeled the carpet back, revealing glossy wooden floors.

"They're clean, Roxy! Look!" There were a few specks of pink paint here and there, but that wasn't anything we couldn't clean off. We worked for a few hours, with Meli's abuela pointing out the spots we missed. The room would need new paint, but it was looking okay again.

"We did it!" Benji said, and Ben high-fived him.

"What do you think, Meli?" I asked. "Do you think Evy and Dad will make up?"

Meli was about to say something when her grandmother came back into the room. She was holding a single sheet of notebook paper with something written on it. "It's not going to be that simple, niños. Miren." She held out the paper for us to look at. Meli and I locked eyes—Evy's mysterious list! It read:

1) No discipline

2) No veggies, ever

3) Hygiene

4) The girls can't stand each other

5) Money-pit house

"That's my daughter," Meli's abuela said with a sigh. "She sees problems so clearly, but not always the solutions."

Evy had spelled it all out, hadn't she? This was a list of all the ways our families were different. Too different, in fact. And maybe number four wasn't true anymore, but the rest of it was. Dad hardly ever set any rules, and it was true, we ate a lot of junk food. The vacuum at our old house broke years ago and Dad never even replaced it. As for the money-pit house? It was already a mess, way before Meli and I made it worse.

"Wait!" Benji said, poking at the paper in his grandmother's hands. He tugged it loose and flipped it over. "There's more to the list."

6) Carlos is a great father

7) The boys adore each other

8) Meli needs someone spontaneous like Roxy

9) Roxy needs someone careful like Meli

10) We all need each other, not in spite of our differences, but <u>BECAUSE</u> of them!

Evy had underlined the last point on her list and drew hearts around the word *because*.

I snatched the paper and read the list again—the good side and the bad side. "Do you think Dad only read the first part of the list?"

"I think so!" Meli said breathlessly.

"Just like you and me, Meli," I said quietly. Meli's mouth opened and she nodded. I didn't have to explain further. She understood what I meant.

"We believed all the wrong things about each other."

"And now Dad and Evy are doing the same thing!"

"That's it, then!" Ben shouted, smacking his forehead. "We show Dad the good list and then everything will be better! Then Dad and Evy will make up, just like you and Meli."

I shook my head. "I don't think it'll be that easy. Dad and Evy believe the bad list because they've had lots of proof. Look around. We need to prove to them that Evy's good list is right."

"The Building Plan," Benji whispered.

"The Building Plan," Ben repeated.

Meli turned in place and took in the room. She had a look on her face that reminded me of the Miami Dolphins' greatest quarterback, Dan Marino. He used to play before I was even born, but I've seen videos of the way he rallied his team to a perfect season. There was always a twinkle in his eye. That twinkle was shining in Meli's eyes now.

"Let's have it, Captain," I said. "What's the plan?"

"We bring it all together—house AND family. Remember all those broken tiles?"

"The really colorful ones?" I asked.

Meli nodded. "I have an idea. As for the rest of it, I think we are going to need reinforcements." She bit the side of her lip and looked at me hesitantly. "Do you mind if I ask James and Janette to help?"

"Mind? Are you kidding me? We need all the help we can get!"

Meli let out a sigh. "But we have to hurry. I

peeked at Mami's phone and she's already written up her 'Sorry, wedding's canceled' email. But it's still in her drafts folder!"

"We have to fix everything before she hits send," I added.

I watched as Meli texted her friends and thought about mine. I could hear the goblin trying to tell me that Meli didn't like Lucia and Camila, but now I knew it wasn't telling the truth. "I could ask my friends to come over too."

"That'd be great!"

"Great!" I echoed.

Meli put away her phone. "Now how do we stall your dad?"

"Easy," I said. "I told him we would be at the library. They're having a summer reading party today and tomorrow until closing time. It's where Ben and I have been going while Dad's been at work the last few days."

"It's been wonderful," Ben said, a dreamy look in his eyes. At the rate he was going, he'd soon finish all the books in the kids' section.

"Perfect," Meli said. Then, she faced her grandmother. "Abuela, you have to keep my mom away until we're ready."

"Consider it done," she said. Then Meli's abuela smiled at her. "You know, mi vida, you remind me of my own mother, your bisabuela, Chela. Chela kept our family together in dark times. She gave it her all. And here you both are," she said, and looked at me too, "preserving your family. You may not be sisters by blood, but you're sisters of the heart. Hermanas del corazón." She stroked my hair and patted Meli's cheek.

"Te quiero, Abuela," Meli whispered.

Abuela dropped a kiss on each of our heads, and off she went. We watched her go. Then, Meli reached out her hand.

"We start in the garden," she said.

I put my hand in hers. "Together," I said.

"Together," Meli echoed.

CHAPTER 17
MELI

"Does everyone have their list?" I asked as we pulled into the home improvement store parking lot the next morning.

"Check!" the Benjamins yelled.

"Got it!" Roxy said, holding up an already crumpled note.

Abuela simply nodded and smiled at me as she turned off the car. Kiwi huffed and shook her head, her ears flapping loudly.

"Remember. In and out. No dillydallying. We don't have a lot of time," I said. Mami was off looking at apartments again, but she'd be back at Abuela's by dinnertime, and Roxy calculated that we'd have plenty of time before the library's summer reading party was over and her dad got off work. This meant it was only a matter of hours before our parents started wondering what we were up to.

"Daylight's a-wasting!" Roxy said, placing Kiwi in the orange shopping cart. A burst of air-conditioning greeted us as we stepped through the sliding doors and our little group disbanded. Abuela and the boys headed toward the paint section while Roxy, Kiwi, and I made our way to the wood-and-tiles section.

"Remember the last time we were here?" Roxy said. "How you tipped over the box of nails and they scattered everywhere?" Her shoulders shook as she giggled quietly.

"Omg! Or how you had the whole store looking for you, calling your name over the PA system? 'Roxana Romero, please meet your parents at the customer service desk. . . .'" I made my voice sound like a robotic grown-up, but I couldn't get all the words in without laughing so hard I snorted.

"So embarrassing!" she gasped. "I'm surprised they let us back in here."

"Yeah." My amusement settled down into nervousness with a sigh. It wasn't that long ago that we'd walked through these doors with a plan to tear our families apart. Now we were going down the aisles looking for just the right tools and supplies to piece us back together.

"I really hope this works," Roxy said as if she'd just read my mind.

"It has to."

We filled the shopping cart with a plank of wood, protective goggles for our eyes, heavy-duty gloves, a couple of hammers, super glue, and a clipper-looking thing called a nipper, which is what Janette had told us we'd need when I texted the JMJ group chat about our plan. Then we went looking for grout. Grabbing one end each, we lifted two bags onto the bottom of the cart.

I checked the items off our list. "That just leaves one last thing."

"The most important one," Roxy said. "Fingers crossed they have it."

It wasn't looking too promising. The nursery had a zillion different varieties of ceramic planters and white plant pots in every size, but they were all shaped like vases and not the very specific shape we were looking for. I could tell Roxy was starting to get anxious because she picked up her pace, pulling the shopping cart from the front of the basket while I kept my hands on the handlebar, trying to keep up.

"It has to be perfect, it has to!"

The way she said *perfect* reminded me of Mami, and in a lot of ways, me. I was always rolling my eyes at how Mami tried to keep everything in order, everything under control in her planner, but in the end, hadn't that just made things worse? If she hadn't written down all those things about the Romeros, and if Carlos had only flipped to the back of the list instead of literally only looking on the negative side, they'd still be together, and everyone would be happy. I thought of how obsessed I'd been with getting every little detail right for the talent show, and how upset I'd been when Roxy's balloons interrupted my presentation. And I had *definitely* not been okay when Papi changed our Legoland plans.

Still, yesterday morning at Dr. Moss's, Mami hadn't fretted over the two new degrees in my spine's curvature. Instead of focusing on her worries, she'd focused on making me feel better. It was so sweet of her, so . . . Carlos-like.

"Maybe it doesn't have to be perfect," I said. All this time, I'd been so afraid of change that it made me put my guard up. I'd assumed the worst in people, Roxy especially, instead of seeing us all for the pretty awesome family we could be.

"What do you mean?"

I steered the shopping cart toward the aisle where they kept the big storage containers, but not before I grabbed two cans of brown and gold spray paint along the way. We stopped in front of a heavy-duty yellow plastic box that had a lid flipped open like a treasure chest.

"It's not exactly what we pictured, but we'll make

it ours," I said. "We'll paint it and decorate it and—"

"It's better than perfect," Roxy said. "It's perfectly us."

Back at the house, the boys were unloading the supplies they'd picked out with Abuela. There were cans of paint, extra-strong tape, and a tarp to cover the floor that could've come in handy days ago in our rooms, if we hadn't, you know, purposely destroyed the carpet.

Roxy put on her gloves and goggles and rubbed her hands together. "Okay, now all we need to get started is—"

Abuela's phone rang. "It's Evy! On FaceTime! Quick!" she said. "Find a wall that looks like my house so she doesn't realize we're at this house when I answer!"

We scrambled from room to room while the phone kept ringing. It was no use! The fixer-upper was too unique. No other house looked like it.

"Can't you just send her to voicemail?" I yelled from the pantry.

"And worry your mother even more?" Abuela yelled back.

"We've got it!" Ben shouted from the kitchen. He and Benji were standing on two chairs, arms outstretched to hold up a white bed sheet against our pastel-green wall. "Now it looks white, like your bedroom!"

Abuela looked skeptical, but there was really no time to second-guess it. She stood in front of the sheet, hit answer, and yelled, "¿Alo? ¿Como vas, hija?"

"Mami? Where are you?"

"Home."

"Is that . . . a sheet behind you?" Mami asked.

"Oh, that?" Abuela laughed nervously.

Roxy started waving her arms around behind the phone, trying to get Abuela's attention as she started what looked like a game of Charades.

"Oh, I was just . . ."

Roxy balled up both hands and rubbed them together.

"Boxing . . . ?"

Roxy shook her head and made like she was wringing a piece of fabric.

"I mean, I was doing laundry!" Abuela said. "Yes, laundry."

Roxy nodded excitedly and mimed hanging something on a line to dry.

"I like air-drying the sheets," Abuela added. "It's more natural."

"Um. Okay," Mami said. "Anyways, I just wanted to let you know how my meeting went with the new Realtor. She's really excited about listing the house. She's coming by to photograph it tomorrow morning."

Ben's jaw dropped. Benji mouthed TO-MOR-ROW?! The sheet they held shook a little.

"Tomorrow? ¿Tan pronto?" Abuela said. "Pero all your boxes are still here—I mean, there."

"The sooner the better, I think. I'll be home in a few hours. ¿Cómo están Meli y Benji?"

"Muy bien. They went to the park. A caminár con Kiwi," Abuela said. At the sound of *walk* in Spanish, Kiwi started twirling in happy circles, causing her dog tag to jingle super loud. I scooped her up before Mami could hear it. "Okay bueno, nos vemos!" Abuela hung up before Mami could say another word. "Oof! That was close, chicos. Let's get this done before she's onto us."

Benji dropped his arms and rubbed his muscles, sore from holding the sheet up. "It's no use. We'll never finish in time." That hopeful look on his face that'd been keeping me afloat all morning was gone.

"That's not true," Roxy said. "We called for reinforcements, remember? They'll be here any minute."

As if on cue, the doorbell rang, and sure enough there was Lucia and Camila looking like they'd just done warm-up drills, bursting with energy. I said hi and thanked them for coming to help. To be honest, though, I was in shock. A good kind of shock. I could see why Roxy was so into sports—her teammates were ready to help one another through anything.

"Do you have one of those?" I asked Roxy, pointing at the jerseys with nicknames on the back.

Roxy grinned and nodded. Then she started going around the room giving everyone high fives when suddenly she yelled, "James! Janette! You're here!"

My breath caught as I said hi and braced myself for things to get awkward. After all, I'd spent so much time complaining to James and Janette about Roxy, they probably thought she was the worst.

"We're happy to help. Meli's been so down ever since your parents split," James said to Roxy.

"Yeah, I thought she was going to start texting me pictures of you two, that's how much she missed you," Janette added.

"Seriously. And I'm really sorry I told Meli to go all out on the Disaster Planning. We just thought you two hated each other, and, well, we might've gotten carried away being Team Meli," James said, looking at me and smiling.

Roxy laughed. "I get it. Team Meli *is* pretty cool," she said.

"So's Team Roxy," I added, and instead of feeling nervous that my friends would clash if my worlds collided, I felt like my world was getting bigger and happier. They smiled and nodded as Roxy showed them where the paint supplies were and what colors would go where.

The boys joined Lucia and Camila in our parents' room and started rolling out the tarp over the floor.

The thick, giant plastic sounded like thunder, and when I peeked inside all I saw were the two blue silhouettes as the Bens held the tarp over their heads, trying to stretch it from one wall to the other. Abuela laughed and took pictures.

"I can't believe it's all coming together," I said. Roxy and I grabbed our yellow storage container and brought it to where Janette was setting up on the patio.

"This is going to be great," Janette said. She began sifting through the pieces of tile Mami and Carlos had broken, picking out a wide assortment of colors. In Ms. Ledero's art club, this had been Janette's specialty, and I could tell she was enjoying getting to teach us. "Now watch. This is a very technical part, so you have to do it carefully." Then she covered several tiles with a drop cloth and started hammering at them randomly. Roxy and I giggled, excited to give it a try ourselves. Janette handed us the hammer.

"Who wants to go first?"

"I think Roxy should do it," I said. "Make something beautiful from all the wreckage."

CHAPTER 18
ROXY

Meli was on fire. Not literally, of course. She was aflame with *artistic inspiration*. After we broke all the tiles into pieces, Meli laid them down on the concrete patio, piece by piece, as she planned her design.

I started painting the plastic tub with brown paint. I wished I had Meli's talent for art. Twice, she stopped what she was doing to give me some direction. Just a few days ago, that would have bugged me. I would have thought: *There goes Meli, telling me how I'm not perfect.* I would have snapped at her, and she would have bit back. Now I knew she was just trying to be helpful, and Meli would end each suggestion with, "What do you think?"

By the time I was finished, the plastic storage tub looked like an ancient wooden chest. At least it did from a distance.

"Green, gold, and red pieces on top," Meli muttered to herself as she worked. "And the mosaic goes inside," she said, then puffed a lock of hair from the front of her face. Carefully, she transferred the tiles to the "treasure chest," nudging them into place with the tip of her finger.

"It looks so cool," I said, standing up to take the mosaic in.

"Do you think they'll like it?" Meli asked nervously.

I took a deep breath. "I really, really hope so."

"There," Meli said, putting in the last piece. Then, she closed the box. We stood to admire our creation.

A crash from inside the house caught our attention and we ran to check on the others.

As we stepped back into the house, I realized we were nowhere near getting the place in good shape. The plan had been simple: We'd show our parents the house tomorrow, demonstrate what a great team we were, and inspire them to make up before that *other* Realtor came.

But the truth was, parts of the house were worse than when we'd started! And the reinforcements we'd called in were making a mess! Janette was standing in the kitchen, a jar of marinara shattered at her feet. There was red sauce everywhere, including in Janette's hair.

"I think I broke it," she said.

"You *think* you broke it?" I asked.

"I think you somehow *exploded* it," Meli added.

Just then, Lucia and James began arguing over who got to use the vacuum and accidentally busted open the dust canister. Soon everyone was sneezing, plus the floors were dirty. Again.

Meli rubbed her face. "We should have invited our friends over when we were in Disaster Plan mode."

"This is going to backfire."

"Let's not think like that. We're giving it our best." Through the open windows we could hear Abuela shouting, "Niños! Leave the power washer alone, por Dios!"

Just then, we heard the Bens whooping and hollering.

"Now what?" Meli groaned, and we ran just in time to see what they'd done to Carlos and Evy's bedroom.

"It's . . . purple!" I shouted. One of the walls was almost fully colored! Meanwhile, the paint cans with the sophisticated shade of beige that Evy had picked out were on the ground, still sealed.

"Yeah!" said Benji. "I found these cans of purple paint in the garage."

"The old owners probably left them behind," Ben said. His arms were crossed and he was looking at the wall like it was a masterpiece.

I spun slowly around the room. At least it was only half of a wall. We could probably cover it up in beige in no time—

"What's that?" Meli shouted, pointing to the ceiling. I looked up. Was the ceiling . . . crumbling? I squinted. Hundreds of tiny, grayish wads of paper were stuck up there. One of them fell on my forehead.

It was damp.

"Spitballs," Benji said. "I got bored while Ben painted."

"Ew!" I cried, wiping my face with my sleeve. "Benji, that is so gross!"

Benji gave me a hug. "Sorry, Roxy. At least you don't have a spitball stuck up your nose," he said, then pinched his nostrils a few times.

"Wait. Is there a spitball up your nose?" Meli asked, worried. She made a concerned expression that was all Evy.

"Yup," Benji said. "Don't ask me how it got there in the first place." Then he sneezed a spitball into the palm of his hand. "Got it," he said.

What a mess this is, I thought. I couldn't believe it. We'd finally done it. We'd created an actual disaster.

I followed Meli out of the room. She slumped on the couch and I sat beside her. It felt like we were sitting in the still eye of a hurricane while all around us our friends, brothers, Abuela, and Kiwi were swirling around us, making bigger and bigger messes that we would never be able to clear up.

"Are you all right?" Meli asked.

"I think so," I said. "How about you?"

Meli shrugged. "I think the Building Plan is doomed. When Carlos and Mami see the house, they're going to be angrier than ever."

It was hard to argue against it. But I knew that, no matter what happened, we had grown something unexpected that summer. Something special that nobody could have predicted.

I put my head on Meli's shoulder. "If this doesn't work, I promise to be your sister no matter what. It'll be true in my heart, anyway."

"Me too. Hermanas del corazón," Meli whispered.

The doorbell rang and we both sat up, startled. Meli's abuela went up to the peephole to see who it was.

"Ay, dios mio. ¡Niños! Come quick!"

She opened the door and there stood Dad and Evy, arms crossed, wearing the biggest frowns I'd ever seen.

CHAPTER 19
MELI

Talk about a domino effect. The second we saw Mami and Carlos standing at the front door, Benji yelled, "Mami?" so loud that it startled James, who hit his head on the shelf he was fixing, which made all the tools he'd been using crash to the ground. All at once, an awkward hush came over the house, as if everyone knew we were in big trouble. Our parents stepped inside and walked to opposite ends of the living room.

"Um, surprise!" Camila waved at them.

"Shhh," Lucia whispered, standing frozen still.

"Hey, guys? I think we should go outside. To the trampoline," Janette said. We watched our friends scoot and bump into one another as they clumsily set down their tools and left the room, mumbling in confusion as they went.

Roxy slipped her hand into mine and squeezed. Our palms were sweaty, and I could feel my heart pounding faster and faster in my chest. I squeezed back as hard as I could, hoping it would telepathically tell her, *It'll be okay. We've got this.* But I wasn't so sure.

"What is this?" Mami said, once it was just our family. "What is going on? We've been worried sick. You girls don't pick up your phones—"

"And Roxy? Ben? The library called and said you never checked in! Since when do we sneak around in this family?" Carlos scanned the room and ran his hands through his hair, looking like he might pull it all out.

"¡Y Mamá! How could you enable them?" Mami said to Abuela.

"¡Enable ni que enable! The kids were determined. They were going to do something with or without me." She crossed her arms and shrugged, looking around the room. "At least with me here they didn't break any bones or burn down the house."

From beside me, I heard Ben's tiny voice mumble, "We came close."

As quick as I could, I put my arm around him and patted him on the shoulder. "He's kidding! He's such a kidder."

Our parents weren't having it. The cracks on the ceiling had a better chance of forming a smile than their mouths did.

"Melisa Clarita Flores, what were you thinking?" Mami finally said.

All day long I'd been practicing the mini speech I'd give our parents, which included a list of the reasons we should be together again, but nothing could've prepared me for this. I tried anyway. "We needed you to see the house again, see that we—"

But Mami wasn't listening. "Get your things. We're leaving."

"No! You can't make us!" Benji plopped down on the floor with his legs crossed.

My jaw dropped. Benji never talked back to Mami. She gasped, just as shocked.

"Evy, hijita," Abuela said. "The kids' hearts are in the right place. Hear them out."

"It took us nearly all day, but we cleaned the floors," Ben said, but all we had to show for it was a dirty dustpan and a mop that'd been dropped in the middle of the room.

"Yeah! And we painted your bedroom," Benji added, pointing across the hall, where the loud purple glared at us.

Mami shook her head. "I know you tried, kids. But this isn't one of those home improvement shows where everything comes out perfectly in thirty minutes."

Oh no, I thought. *She's using her calm voice.* This meant she was about to let us down gently.

"I get it. We messed up," Roxy said. "Please, let us fix it."

Carlos took off his glasses. Normally this would be the moment when he'd hug Roxy and reassure her everything was going to be all right. Instead he turned to them and said, "Roxana. Benjamin. This has gone too far."

Evy placed her hand on his arm. "Carlos, go easy on them."

"No, you were right. I don't give them enough discipline. And sure, the girls are getting along, *for now*. And this house! It *is* a money pit, an endless money pit. You were right, Evy, about all of it."

"All of it?" she said. "You mean my list?"

"But he didn't *read* all of it!" Benji cried, with so much ganas it was like hearing him yell *UNO!* at the end of a game.

Mami took a step closer to Carlos. "Is that true?"

"What difference does it make?" he said, taking a step back.

"Reading the whole list makes *all* the difference!" Roxy said. "Because those things are true, but only in the good ways! I know Meli and I have fought a lot this summer, but it's because we care so much about each other and didn't even know it. She understands me and helps me understand myself better, even when we let the hard things we're going through in our lives come between us. But I'm never going to let that happen again,

I promise. We need each other! Not just Meli and me, but the Benjamins too! They're like the sun and the moon: complete opposites but they light up our sky. And you two! Dad, Evy. I don't *really* think it's gross when you hug and kiss. I think it's sweet and sometimes cheesy, but only because you're so obviously in love. You bring out the best in each other, and that makes all of us super lucky because it means you're even cooler parents together than you are apart."

Tears were streaming down her cheeks now, and mine too. Here I'd been, worried about my speech, when Roxy just said everything I wanted to say and more. I brought my T-shirt up to wipe away the wetness piling around my neck.

Our parents locked eyes.

This was it. The moment everything would click.

"This is too much," Carlos mumbled.

"I can't do this here," Mami said at the same time.

He walked out of the room and into the backyard, and Mami followed.

James, Jannette, Lucia, and Camila came back into the living room as soon as our parents stepped outside.

"They seemed like they wanted some privacy," James said, raising an eyebrow. "You and Roxy okay?"

I shrugged. "I just wish I knew what they were talking about." But this wasn't like our usual schemes when we might find a way to eavesdrop on them. It had to be different this time.

Abuela offered us all juice boxes while we waited. Eventually, when our friends got so bored they started competing over who could make the loudest slurping sounds with their straws, we suggested they go for a walk down to the park. Roxy went around giving everyone hugs and thanking them for their help, but all I could muster was to wave at them from the corner of the room. Once the last of them had left, Roxy slid down the wall and sat on the floor next to me, placing her head on my shoulder. The light coming through the windows had turned orange now that the sun was setting.

"Chicos, chicas!" Carlos called for us to come out to the backyard.

"Finally!" Roxy said. The four of us ran and found our parents by the garden, standing next to our open treasure chest.

"What is the meaning of this?" Mami said, pointing at the mosaic. She looked puzzled by all the shattered pieces.

"You explain," Roxy whispered.

"No, *we* tell them," I said. "There's pieces of all of us in here." I took a deep breath and started by pointing out the clusters of brown and white tiles in the shape of an oval.

"That's a football! For me!" Roxy said.

"Exactly. Because you're the captain. A leader. You motivate me," I said.

She patted the top of my head. "And that's Meli. The seashell."

I nodded and shrugged. "I wasn't sure what to put. So I took inspiration from my scoliosis sculpture."

"It totally works. Shells are delicate and sensitive, but also strong."

"Thanks." I loved how Roxy noticed things I wouldn't have thought of myself.

"And those two dinosaurs are us, right?" Ben said.

I nodded. "Guess which one's which."

"The pterodactyl with the wings, that's Benji's favorite," Ben said.

"Yup. Because he's always soaring above us, full of energy." I thought I heard Mami giggle, but I was too nervous to look at her.

"And that long-necked one is a brachiosaurus. Ben's favorite," Benji said.

"That's perfect," Roxy said. "Because he's our gentle giant."

The boys ran their fingers over the mosaic. Individually the pieces didn't look like much more than broken tile, but together they became something wonderful. Even when they didn't fit perfectly, the spaces between them, where the cement was, created a bond.

"Mira, that's you," Carlos said to Mami. "The clock."

I was relieved he could see it. That had been the hardest shape to make.

"Because I'm always on our case about being punctual?"

"No. Because you're the steady one. We can always count on you to keep us on track," I said.

"Ay, Meli." Mami wrapped her arms around me from behind.

"Wait a second, am I this green one?" Carlos said. "Is that . . . Kermit the frog?"

"Don't be mad!" I said. "I mean it in the best way. You're the laid-back, cheerful one who just wants us all to be happy."

"It's true, mi amor. Kermit keeps everyone's spirits up, always," Mami said.

Mi amor?! Did she just call him mi amor?

Roxy turned to look at me, her lips curved in a smile but squeezed together like a zipper she was trying not to burst open. If our parents were using pet names again, did this mean . . . ?

"I'm at a loss for words, kids," Carlos said. "This mosaic, the house."

"It's beautiful," Mami said.

"Bueno, this is beautiful." Carlos gestured at the backyard. "The inside of the house, on the other hand? Eso es un arroz con mango."

We all laughed. He wasn't wrong. It was total chaos in there, just like a plate full of rice and mangos all mixed up together.

Mami slipped her hand into Carlos's. "But it has a lot of love."

Our parents turned to face each other, and I'm pretty sure the four of us kids stopped breathing at the same exact time, waiting for them to kiss or hug or do *anything*. But they just smiled and seemed to be on another planet altogether.

Ben squirmed and gasped. "I can't take the suspense! Does this mean we're a family again?"

Carlos laughed. Mami gave him the tiniest nod, and he leaned forward to kiss her.

"Well?" Roxy yelled. "Use your words!"

I nodded, not wanting to get too excited until it was official.

"Yes, mis amores," Mami said. "We're back together again."

"All six of us," Carlos added as he put his arms over me and Roxy's shoulders. Behind him, she and

I linked hands and started doing little hops. The boys tackled Mami around the waist.

"We did it!" Benji said.

Roxy squeezed my arm. "Can you believe it?"

"No! But also yes!" Things had turned out nothing like we'd planned—disaster or building—but somehow, they felt right in ways I'd never imagined. We walked back inside as a family.

Roxy twirled a scrunchie around her wrist, looking up at the ceiling as if she was trying real hard to think of something. "This is better than that time our class won the hacky sack relay race during Field Day."

"Better than a new blank canvas," I added.

"Better than a sundae with extra fudge and rainbow sprinkles!" Benji said.

"The best, like when you find the last piece of a puzzle and it's finally complete," Ben said, smiling timidly at each of us. I met his eyes and smiled back.

We watched as Abuela congratulated our parents in the living room. She teased them that she knew all along, the second she saw them ringing the doorbell to their own house, that they'd get back together.

"Well, how else was I supposed to get inside? You had my key, remember?" Mami said.

"And as soon as I thought Roxy and Ben were up to something, I left the hotel so fast I forgot my keys," Carlos said.

Even Kiwi joined in on the celebration, scratching at Carlos's heels and wagging her tail.

"She likes you," Abuela said. "You know, she'd make a good flower girl."

"Yes, but let's focus on fixing the house before we start fitting Kiwi for dresses," Mami said.

I'd never heard so much laughter in one room. It's true that in our old house it had always been the four of us: Benji, Mami, Papi, and me: the Floreses. And for a time after my parents broke up, I thought we'd been split apart, when maybe all along we were just branching off like a tree, making room for our family to grow in all the ways it needed to be happiest.

"Bueno, mi viejita Mirta has a cousin whose sister-in-law knows a guy who owns a construction company," Abuela said to Carlos. "He can probably get this house move-in ready in a matter of weeks."

"Thank you. That's very nice of Mirta," Carlos said. "But we have some contractors ready to start. I'm thinking this time we stay at the hotel till the house is ready, que les parece?" he said to me and Roxy.

"Another vacation before school starts? Sign me up!" Roxy said.

"Meli! Ben! Roxy! Benji! Vengan, let's take a picture," Mami said.

Abuela took out her phone and started directing us where to go. In a matter of seconds, Roxy and I had sat in the middle of the sofa, the Benjamins sat with their legs crossed in front of us on the floor, Mami and Carlos sat on the sides, and Kiwi jumped into my lap.

Roxy locked her arm with mine. "It's our first family portrait."

Then in a louder voice, she called out to the rest of the group. "Say *familia*!"

"FAMILIA!!" we shouted.

We gathered around the phone to look at the picture. Behind us, the house was still in shambles. But in the center? We were all smiles in our new home.

Part Four:

~~Never~~ Forever Sisters

CHAPTER 20
ROXY

"What do you mean you lost the rings?" Meli asked. There was a note of panic in her voice.

Ben and Benji, dressed in their matching wedding-day suits, both slowly pointed a finger at each other.

"It's his fault!" they said at the same time.

Benji gasped. "Tying the rings to Kiwi's collar was your idea!"

"But you're the one who did it. And now Kiwi is missing!" cried Ben.

Meli went pale. "What do you mean you lost Kiwi?"

Again, the boys pointed at each other. Meli lunged at them, but I held her back by the waist.

"She's probably hiding under a blanket, like she always does. Let's go find her."

The house was full of people getting ready for Dad and Evy's wedding. Abuela had taken over the kitchen with the help of her domino-playing viejitas, and the whole house smelled sweet. A tower of picarones in chancaca syrup dominated one end of the kitchen counter. I had already eaten four before Abuela stopped me. Outside, guests sat on folding chairs, waiting for the ceremony to begin.

It had been seven weeks since Meli and I cooked up the Disaster-Turned-Building Plan, but it felt like forever ago. Eventually, with the help of the contractors, the house was cleaned up and livable again. Eventually. While the pros worked on the money-pit house, we left the *do-it-yourself*-ing to the wedding tasks. So Meli and I turned in our Disaster Plan hats for Wedding Planner ones. Meli designed her junior bridesmaid dress herself, sewing layers of delicate tulle in different pastels to form the skirt and bodice. She made sure to add pockets to her dress. I picked my dress off the rack—it was aqua all over—and

I pinned a bright orange orchid in my hair. It had pockets, too, which was the best part, and the fabric was in the Miami Dolphins' colors, of course!

"We have to find the rings before Mami and Carlos go down the aisle!" Meli said. Just then, Kiwi ran between us, the rings dangling from a shoelace tied to her collar.

"Catch that dog!" I yelled, and the two of us, followed by the Bens, tore through the house.

"Ay!" Abuela shouted, as Kiwi zipped between her feet and ran for the open front door.

I dove for the ground just before Kiwi could escape. "Gotcha!" I shouted in triumph.

"Roxy saves the day!" cheered Benji, and I smiled so big it felt like my cheeks would get stuck that way.

"Good job, sis," Meli said, then started straightening my dress as I stood.

I brushed her hands away. "Quit it, quit it." Meli would always want everything to be perfect, just like Evy. I was okay with things being a little bit messy, like my Dad. And that was okay.

"Sorry. You look supercute," she said.

"You too! We may be on special teams today, but everyone's going to notice us anyway," I said.

Meli's brow furrowed. "Sometimes it's like you're speaking a different language, you know that?"

I slung my arm around her shoulders. "You'll get it eventually."

I untied the rings from Kiwi's collar and handed one to each of the Bens. "Keep them safe this time," I said, and they both nodded solemnly. Meli straightened Benji's bow tie, which was made of Lego bricks. Their Papi had come through on the Legoland trip after all. Ben's bow tie was lavender-colored and a gift from Mom, who had moved back to Miami a few weeks ago. She was happier than she'd been in a long time, and Ben and I spent every other weekend with her, just like we used to.

Also? I hadn't heard from the goblin in my brain in a long time.

At my last appointment, Dr. Nordan told me how proud she was of me, and how much I'd grown since we'd first met. I high-fived her so hard she nearly toppled off her chair.

Evy had made a bouquet for herself, and smaller ones for me and Meli. They each had beautiful pink *flores* in them, and sprigs of fragrant *romero*—a perfect combination of our family names. Evy wore a strapless dress and a pink hibiscus flower tucked behind her ear, while Dad wore a white tuxedo with matching hibiscus flowers printed on the lapel. The six of us lined up at the sliding glass door that opened to the backyard.

"Listos?" Dad asked.

"Listos!" we all said.

Music started playing and everyone seated in the folding chairs turned to watch. Lucia and Camila were seated beside James and Janette. They were talking, then suddenly, Camila turned around, caught my eye, and told the others to look. The four of them waved at us. I wiggled my fingers back at them and Meli blew them all a kiss. My stomach did a couple of somersaults, but I knew it was because I was excited, not nervous.

"On the count of three," Evy said softly. "One, two—"

"Kiwi, no!" Meli said, just as Kiwi tore down the path, kicking up dirt with her tiny paws. All the guests seated next to the aisle lifted their feet as the tiny Yorkie came crashing by. There were gasps and laughter, and many people used their phones to snag a photo of Kiwi. The dog ran right up to the officiant, who happened to be my uncle Al, and sat beside him.

I turned, worried that Evy would be flipping out, but she was laughing so hard tears had sprung from her eyes.

"Well, we know who's in charge in this family," Dad said. He didn't have to spell it out, but he did: "Kiwi!"

Evy and Dad got married in front of all our friends and loved ones out in the backyard, saying their vows and promising to love each other and to love us too, no matter what. Uncle Al pronounced them husband and wife, then turned to us and said, "And I pronounce you sisters and brothers! Congratulations!"

Ben and Benji jumped to their feet and clapped,

shouting "Woo-hoo!" The guests all went *aw* and took more pictures. Meli took my hand in hers and squeezed and I squeezed back.

There was a time I'd thought becoming sisters with Meli would change my life in all the worst ways. I hadn't imagined she and Benji and Evy could change our lives by becoming family.

And that's what we were now—legally, in fact!

Before we knew it, the ceremony was over. Dad and Evy smooched and I looked away. I didn't think I'd ever get used to *that*. They walked down the path between the folding chairs, headed to the white tent where there would be wedding cake to eat, and songs to dance to.

I got up to go to the tent too when Meli suddenly grabbed my wrist. I watched as she signaled to the Bens, and we followed her to the garden, where the treasure chest we'd created still sat in pride of place.

"We should make some vows too," Meli said. She wore a serious look, and I could tell she'd been thinking about this for a long time. "I'll go first. I promise to be patient with the Bens, even when they come into my room without permission. And I promise to try to understand football for Roxy, and to never, ever jump to conclusions when we argue."

Benji spoke up next. "The two of us promise to be the best brothers you'll ever have."

Grinning, Ben agreed. "What he said."

"Good enough for me." I'd never made a vow before. I held Meli's hand and Ben's too. Then Benji completed the circle. Behind us, a song began playing—Dad and Evy's first dance. "I'd better make this quick. The party is starting without us. I promise to be there for all of you, even when things are . . ." I paused, searching for the right word.

"Disasters," Meli said, finishing my sentence.

I nodded. "Yes, even then." The boys took off for the tent as soon as we all let go of one another. They ran into Dad and Evy, interrupting their dance. Dad picked Benji up and swung him around while Evy waltzed with Ben.

"Well," Meli asked, "how'd we do?"

"We almost forgot one part!" I slipped my hand into my pocket and pulled out the two mood rings

I'd bought in the Everglades souvenir shop. I handed one to Meli. "I meant to give it to you the day I got it, but then we sort of got into a fight. But I'd like you to have it now. It's like Dad and Evy's rings. A symbol of us."

Meli laughed and slipped the ring on. I did the same.

"Twinning," she said as our rings each turned the same bright blue color. "What does blue mean?"

"Blue means happy."

"Then it's accurate! My turn," Meli said, and reached into her own pocket. Out came a gleaming necklace with a heart-shaped pendant. "It's for you. I won it at the fair."

"The same day I got the rings!"

"Mm-hmm." She poured the necklace into the palm of my hand. "Go on. Open it."

I clicked open the heart and inside were two pictures—one of me on the left, and one of Meli on the right. Words caught in my throat so I couldn't get them out. Meli must have heard them anyway because she pulled me into a giant hug, which made me laugh.

"Come on, I'll help you put it on." Meli worked the clasp at the back of my neck until I heard a tiny click. The locket felt cool and smooth against my skin. I had a sister! Suddenly I felt like the luckiest kid in the world.

Meanwhile, music pounded from the tent, and we watched as Dad and Evy started a conga line and a shout of "¡Wepa!" went up into the air. Together, we headed toward the tent.

"We're official now, sis," Meli said. She had to shout over the party sounds.

"Not that it's a competition or anything, but I think our sibling vows were much better than the grown-up ones," I said.

Meli linked arms with me. "I think Mami and Carlos should have hit us up for tips."

We watched as Evy adjusted Dad's lapel flowers for the millionth time, while he accidentally stepped on the long train of her dress.

"They really do need our help all the time, don't they?" Meli said.

"Constantly."

"Sisters forever?"

Once upon a time, we'd been the no way, never sisters. But not now.

We stepped onto the dancefloor, where Dad, Evy, Ben, and Benji were waving at us. "Forever and ever," I answered, and we joined the party.

ACKNOWLEDGMENTS

Though I'd been a fan of her beautiful books, I hadn't known Natalia long when she asked me about the possibility of co-writing something together. "Let's play!" I answered. And play we did! Before we knew it, Meli and Roxy began to take shape in our notebooks. "Our girls" we called them, and our imaginings and plot-busting sessions became this book you are holding in your hands. But something more than a book came from Natalia's initial question to me. As we wrote about these girls, who grow into friendship and then true sisterhood, I felt a similar transformation. Natalia is not just my co-writer and my great friend, but a true sister of my heart. These words fall short in describing how grateful I am to her. So, I'll keep it simple—Natalia, te quiero mucho! Gracias por todo.

My heartfelt gratitude goes to Jessica Smith, our editor at Aladdin. Thank you for falling in love with Meli and Roxy just as hard as we did! You've helped us bring them to their fullest versions of themselves, which is an editor's greatest gift. And thank you to the entire Aladdin team, as well. Your care in bringing books into the world for young readers is so evident and appreciated!

To Stéphanie Abou, my agent and friend, I'm so glad we're on this ride together. Your wisdom, guidance, humor, and friendship have been such a blessing to me this last decade and counting. Here's to the next adventure!

I want to offer a big hug and thank you to Laura Dail for your support of the *No Way Never Sisters* Team! It's been wonderful working with you.

Over the course of the last few years, I've had the privilege of meeting so many readers, teachers, and media specialists at schools all over. You are all my greatest inspiration! If we've ever met, please know I remember you and treasure the memory. To young readers—keep reading, dreaming, studying, playing, and making things. I am so proud of you all. And to the educators out there—I'm in awe of what you do, and heartened knowing there are so many of you out there, caring for kids and feeding them books to grow on.

I am so grateful to Mitchell Kaplan and the Books & Books Literary Foundation for all you do to serve Miami-Dade children and the future of literacy. Mitchell, you're the literary heart and soul of my hometown. Thanks, as well, to Laura Deutsch and the whole Books & Books family for your excellent support of authors visiting schools.

My beloved family makes my work possible. When I write, I sneak bits and pieces about them into every story because I can't bear to be away from them even in my imagination, even when I'm just one room over and writing away. To Orlando, Penelope, and Mary-Blair—thank you for always being my reason. I love you.

Finally, I dedicate this book to my sister, Andrea. Sissy—I'm so glad our parents fell in love when we were kids and decided to blend our families into a delicious smoothie! Thanks for always being there for us. Oh, how I love you, my forever-ever sister!

—Chantel Acevedo

I have a confession: when it came time to write this book's acknowledgments, my brain shortened the word to "ack!" This felt extremely fitting, because throughout this entire process, I've been so overwhelmed with gratitude that I panic just at the thought of trying to capture my feelings into words. So, dearest of readers, please imagine all my thanks—for you, and everyone in these next pages—multiplied by at least a bajillion. I fear even then, the math may fall short!

First and foremost, to Chantel, for saying "Let's play!" when the idea for this story popped up, and for making it the most fun, joyful, and heartfelt experience I could have ever imagined. Thank you for trusting me in this journey, and most of all, thank you for the magical friendship we've created over months of giddily swapping chapters, brainstorming our girls' schemes, going on bookish road trips, and staying up super late having heart-to-heart chats in our hotel room during our travels—I cherish these moments most of all! Writing with you is an honor (and a blast!), but being your friend is the most beautiful gift that nourishes my spirit. Te quiero mucho, amiga!

To our editor, Jessi Smith, for being Team Roxy and Meli from day one and shaping their story into a book with such care and creativity. Thank you for loving our girls as much as we do. To the entire team at Aladdin, especially Laura Lyn DiSiena for the gorgeous cover design. Merci beaucoup to illustrator Solène Debiès—Meli would definitely be your biggest fan!

With each book my gratitude for my agent, Laura Dail, continues to grow and grow. You have been with me through so many chapters and adventures; thank you for always being game, no matter which direction I go in, and making me feel anything is possible.

Thank you also to Stéphanie Abou for championing this story in every way. Chantel and I got so lucky with the super team that is you and Laura!

To every educator and librarian I've ever met, both as a young student and now as an author: I get to write books because of you. Thank you for nourishing the imaginations of so many of us.

To Barbara Sparrow and Demery Bader-Saye for your constant insights, encouragement, and friendship that have spanned years and miles: I'm endlessly grateful for you. I want to also give a very special shout-out to one of our first readers, Embee! Thank you for coming to Roxy and Meli's first pages with such an open heart and keen eye.

Family is at the heart of this book, and it's the steadfast love, joy, and life-giving laughter of mine that inspires all I do. Thank you to Ursula for always looking out for your little sister. To all of my nieces and nephews: being your aunt is one of my life's greatest joys. To mis primos, for a lifetime of mischief, and to my parents, Ceci and Ramón, mis Nonnos, and mi tía Tere, for embracing us through all of it. And to Kuki, always, for making us each feel like the favorite.

And finally, to mi amor, Eric. Life with you is everything. Thank you for always believing.

—Natalia Sylvester